THE LISTS OF THE PAST

Published by Pharos Editions

Pharos Editions
1752 NW Market Street
308
Seattle WA 98107
www.pharoseditions.com

Except for "Wood" and "Visitors," all of these stories originally appeared in *The New Yorker*.

First edition 1976 by The Viking Press, Inc.

First Pharos Editions Printing May 2014

Pharos Editions version reprinted by arrangement with Charles Blake and Peter Blake

ISBN-13: 9780988172593

SELECTED AND INTRODUCED BY
CHERYL STRAYED

THE LISTS OF THE PAST

Stories by
JULIE HAYDEN

Forward by
S. KIRK WALSH

PHAROS EDITIONS | SEATTLE, WASHINGTON

CONTENTS

INTRODUCTION by Cheryl Strayed XI

FORWARD by S. Kirk Walsh. XIII

BRIEF LIVES

Walking with Charlie. 5

A Touch of Nature. 13

Day-Old Baby Rats 26

Wood 43

Visitors 53

In the Words of. 71

THE LISTS OF THE PAST

The Stories of the House 84

"Eighteen Down" 99

Gardening for Pleasure. 106

Passengers 121

Shut-Eye Night Ride. 133

Under the Weather 154

INTRODUCTION BY
CHERYL STRAYED

It began as things do these days: with a Facebook post. My friend, the poet Cate Marvin, wrote of her admiration for a writer I'd never heard of, a woman named Julie Hayden. Cate had assigned one of Hayden's stories to the students in her college class. When I emailed her and asked her to tell me more, she responded with an urgent tone, imploring me to read Hayden's work, and included a link to a New Yorker fiction podcast of Lorrie Moore reading Hayden's story "Day-Old Baby Rats." The story had been published in *The New Yorker* in January 1972 and three years later it was collected in Hayden's only book—the long out-of-print *The Lists of the Past*.

I clicked play and listened. I sat very still and half held my breath. I was rapt.

In the silence that followed the last line of the story I typed writer Julie Hayden into my computer's search function and was immediately lead to the illuminating essay by S. Kirk Walsh that is reprinted here (it was originally published in the Los Angeles Review of Books). Walsh's piece begins with a retelling of a story essentially like my own—the almost accidental discovery of a writer who had all but been forgotten. Like me, Walsh was stunned. But more, she was compelled to dig deeper. In moving, sad, fascinating detail, Walsh shares details of Hayden's short life that she was able to glean after interviewing Hayden's younger sister, Patsy Hayden

Blake, as well as Elizabeth Macklin, Charles McGrath, and Daniel Menaker, Hayden's colleagues at *The New Yorker*, where she was employed for twelve years in the 1960s and 70s.

A graduate of Radcliffe, the daughter of a poet who was both popular and esteemed—her mother, Phyllis McGinley won the Pulitzer Prize in poetry in 1961 for her book *Times Three*—Hayden committed herself to fiction writing early on, taking notes about the things she felt and observed and crafting stories. In 1970, when Hayden was 31, the first story in this volume, "Walking With Charlie," appeared in *The New Yorker* and in the four years that followed another nine of her stories—all of them in this collection—were published there. They, along with two previously unpublished stories, compose *The Lists of the Past*, which was published by The Viking Press to critical acclaim in 1976.

The acclaim was well-deserved. Hayden's stories are unlike anything I've ever read. Her writing is original and bold, plainspoken and poetic, haunting and profound, merciless and tender. There's a cavernous loneliness at the core of her work—one that echoes the difficulty of her short life, no doubt—but also a vast beauty, one that I believe must also reflect her inner world. It's this intelligent, emotional depth and breadth that ultimately convinced me to select this book for re-issue by Pharos Editions. Hayden isn't just a dazzling writer. She's one who has done the real work of great literature: she has shown us to ourselves. She has reminded us again and anew what it means to be human.

Hayden died of kidney failure at the age of 42, five years after *The Lists of the Past* was published. By then she'd suffered the death of her mother, breast cancer, alcoholism and a long struggle with anxiety that grew debilitating in the final years of her life. What remains is this book, born again in your hands. I hope you'll treasure it.

CHERYL STRAYED

FORWARD BY
S. KIRK WALSH

Julie Hayden's only book, *The Lists of the Past*, was released 36 years ago this summer by The Viking Press. Ten of its stories were originally published in the pages of *The New Yorker*, where Hayden worked for 16 years before her death at age 42.

I discovered Hayden while driving with my husband from Los Angeles to our home in Austin, Texas. For the road trip, I had downloaded multiple podcasts, including several fiction programs from *The New Yorker*. Along a barren stretch of Highway 10 in southeast Arizona, we listened to Lorrie Moore read Hayden's story "Day-Old Baby Rats." The story follows a tormented woman as she wanders the streets and subways of Manhattan, through stores and other public spaces, and finally through the heavy doors of St. Patrick's Cathedral. In the darkness of a confessional, while sipping Scotch from a flask, she tries to ask a priest for help. A slightly older and more broken-down version of Sylvia Plath's Esther Greenwood, Hayden's nameless protagonist embodies the acute loneliness of living in Manhattan—how the distorted lens of irrational fears and past traumas can transform the city into a dangerous landscape, seemingly impossible to navigate.

By the time the story was over, my husband and I had exited the highway and parked outside a diner. Only a few cars were in the lot, which was on a hill overlooking distant mountains. It was an odd and wonderful setting in which to listen to a story that so fully took me back to New York City—where at times during my early twenties I had experienced similar loneliness and intoxication. Over burgers and fries, my husband and

I talked about the emotional power and mastery of the story and how it reminded us of our lost, younger selves. Neither of us could believe that we had never heard of this extraordinary writer.

Returning home, I learned that the book was out of print (and that first editions fetch as much as $240), but was able to locate a copy of *The Lists of the Past* through the interlibrary loan system of my public library. *The Lists of the Past* is divided into two sections: The first, "Brief Lives," tell stories that range from childhood memories during wartime to unrequited affairs of the heart. In "Walking with Charlie," a woman takes her seventeen-month-old nephew to Central Park:

> I feel as though all my life I have been traveling toward this spot, to wait beside this baby at the vortex of his joy. In the spooky silvery light, everything is a clue. There are clues all around me, but I cannot interpret them. I cannot even distinguish the mystery.

In Hayden's careful prose, indelible loss and the opposition of life's natural beauty are closely hemmed together.

The second half of the collection, titled "Lists of the Past," features a series of interconnected stories about a family and the death of its patriarch. Domestic lists jotted down by the father supply a haunting undercurrent throughout much of the narrative. ("Front Porch Stuff, Stain Desk, Apple Tree . . . Drug Stuff, Cokes, Lettuce.") In the concluding story, "Under the Weather," the father's Body and Soul permanently part ways:

> "Don't go," said Body.
>
> "I will," Soul said, and whizzed free as a bird up to a corner of the hospital room, where the male nurse, who was already packing, registered the rattle of his flight, the cessation of the sound of Body breathing, with clinical detachment. He looked at his watch and, closing the lid of the suitcase, went over to the bed.

After reading Hayden's story collection, which stunned me with its vivid brilliance, I couldn't believe that the author was seemingly forgotten. I wanted to learn more about her, so I contacted Hayden's younger sister, Patsy Hayden Blake, and several individuals who had worked with her at the magazine during the seventies. These interviews filled in the tragedy of Julie Hayden's life.

Hayden was the daughter of Pulitzer-prize-winning poet Phyllis McGinley and Bill Hayden, a public relations analyst at Bell Telephone. Blake recalls good times as a family—evenings spent next to the fire, reading Victorian sagas, Edgar Allen Poe, and Robert Louis Stevenson. That said, Blake largely remembers her older sister as an unhappy child. "She had all sorts of fears," says Blake, who now lives with her husband in Santa Barbara. Hayden's fears ran from tall buildings and traveling to escalators and elevators. "I remember during adolescence, my mother saying, 'Try and get a date for your sister,' " Blake says. "And I remember thinking, 'How horrible. How can you expect me to do that?' Julie was not an ordinary girl." Her studies provided a sort of refuge: Hayden attended the Convent of the Sacred Heart in Greenwich and then graduated cum laude in English and ancient Greek from Radcliffe.

After college, Hayden worked at Family Circle before joining the staff of *The New Yorker*. As the newsbreak editor at the magazine, she sifted through hundreds of newspaper clippings that arrived weekly from readers and then sent batches to E.B. White for final selection. "It's one of those jobs that the magazine used to have for people that they liked having around," says poet Elizabeth Macklin, who was William Shawn's secretary during part of Hayden's tenure. "She just wanted to concentrate on her fiction—and it was a good job for that."

According to Blake, her sister wrote all the time, scribbling in twenty-five-cent spiral notebooks that she carried in her pocket, recording her observations of nature, birds, and later her states of suffering. Hayden was an avid birder, with a checklist of over 600 birds despite the fact that she traveled very little. She composed her stories on her mother's portable Royal typewriter. Hayden also spent many summers writing at the MacDowell Colony in Peterborough, New Hampshire.

William Maxwell and his two apprentices at the time—Charles McGrath and Daniel Menaker—served as Hayden's fiction editors. "Julie was hard to edit in the sense that she was very fragile," recalls McGrath, who writes about literature and culture for *The New York Times*. "These stories came with great difficulty and meant so much to her that just the mere suggestion of changing a comma, she would start to tremble and tears would well up in her eyes." At one point, when Maxwell was ill, McGrath chose one of Hayden's stories for an issue of the magazine. "I know the stories rather well," he says. "I knew the stories better than I knew Julie."

The stories were published in the magazine over the next five years before the collection was bought by Viking. Though there was little fanfare at the time of publication, Hayden was very pleased that the book got picked up for review in the daily section and the Sunday Book Review of *The New York Times*. "Julie Hayden's stories . . . comprise a book of illuminations," wrote the critic Richard R. Lingeman, "like a saint's meditation diary." When I recently spoke with Menaker on the phone, he compared her writing to the likes of Anne Beattie, Lorrie Moore, Mary Robison, Deborah Eisenberg, and "in a very remote way, maybe a little like Donald Barthelme."

"During that time, the office was filled with eccentrics," continued Menaker, author most recently of *A Good Talk*. "Considering that she was an original eccentric herself, Julie oddly enough fit in."

Sadly, after the publication of *The Lists of the Past*, Hayden's life spiraled downward. She was diagnosed with breast cancer and underwent surgery, but was too scared to follow through with the prescribed chemotherapy. Her drinking worsened as Hayden attempted to steady her numerous phobias, says Blake. Two years after her diagnosis, her mother passed away. Outward signs of her increasingly troubled state persisted: She grew overweight, rarely showered, and kept odd hours. The magazine asked her to work from home for a stretch of time. "I don't think she saw herself falling apart," remembers Blake. "For us, it was shocking to see her loveliness and wit diminish."

During the remaining months of her life, Hayden became a recluse and starved herself, subsisting on only cans of tuna fish and alcohol. In September of 1981, she was admitted to Columbia Presbyterian and six days later died of kidney failure. The autopsy revealed that her system was riddled with cancer. Her memorial service was held in St. Luke's Gardens in Greenwich Village—a place that Hayden had discovered during a walk in her neighborhood when she was convalescing from surgery and on which she had written an endearing, lengthy profile, published in *The New Yorker* a week before her death. It was her first piece of extended reportorial writing.

"The 'lists' stories stand out for me," says McGrath, "probably because I worked on them, but also because now I feel haunted by them in a way. I think about them all of the time . . . The precision, the eye for the detail, the ability to pack feeling. Those stories are full of feeling without being sappy. She was an original. There was no one else at the magazine writing like that."

Hayden's prose also left a strong impression on Macklin over the years. "It's that sense of absolute bedazzlement," she says of reading "Day-Old Baby Rats" for the first time, "when you are witnessing this thing and you can't even believe it that you had the luck that it came into your hands."

Not long ago, I was visiting my sister in Ann Arbor, Michigan. We spent one day in Detroit and decided to stop by John King Books, the largest used bookstore in Michigan. The giant, four-story factory building overwhelmed me at first, with its endless shelves made of thick plywood and cement bricks, but before long I found myself perusing the fiction section. First, I picked up William Maxwell's *They Came Like Swallows* and then looked for Hayden's *The Lists of the Past*. I was stunned to find an almost-perfect copy for only six dollars. On the inside jacket, a penciled inscription was made out to a woman named Patsy. Readers, I couldn't believe the book landed in my hands.

For Bill Hayden
and all the animals

THE
LISTS OF
THE
PAST

BRIEF LIVES

Walking with Charlie

HAND IN HAND, AND VERY PROPERLY, Charlie and I cross Fifth Avenue as if it were water. In the Saturday-afternoon traffic it is important not to let go; red and green lights are beacons signaling take care, take care. By the time we reach the other side my right hand is moist, and Charlie's, within my fingers, feels cool and amphibious. With my free hand I bump the stroller over the curb; it is stocked with objects his mother has chosen for him: sand toys, several Matchbox cars, *The Gingerbread Man* in a Little Golden Book, a spoon, his crib blanket—extensions of his personality, definitions of street a bored Secret Service man keeps vigil over the apartment house where the children of the late President Kennedy are staying. A low wall separates us from the Park, our destination.

Though familiar with the Park, I am a West Sider. I have identified sixteen kinds of warbler in the Ramble, including the Connecticut, and glimpsed a peregrine falcon menacing children's kites over the Sheep Meadow. The broken kouroi in the Greek Rooms of the museum are old acquaintances; so are the hoarse, ironic seals by the Zoo Cafeteria. But I have usually approached their whereabouts from the west, bicycling through the Park with Robert (who has gone to live in another town), and certainly never before in the company of a seventeen-month-old infant.

It is, in fact, the first time I've ever been alone with Charlie. His landmarks clash upon mine. For a confusing second all directions become jumbled in my mind, and the familiar wavers like a mirage. I cannot remember where I was told to go or what we were to do.

What we are doing right now is watching the shiny, colored cars flow by. City-wise Charlie tallies their passing. " 'N a car," he observes, with an almost blasé flick of the hand I am not holding. " 'N a bus. 'N a tackie car. 'N a car. 'N a car." They are his sheep, or birds. Rumble. Honk. Beep. Screech, they call to him. Before I become mesmerized by the traffic, I choose a direction at random, and at once several mothers with strollers and children appear ahead of us; we follow in their tracks.

Soon we find ourselves at the playground, guarded by bronze gates adorned with figures by Paul Manship, out of Aesop: the fox and the cheese, the lamb and the wolf. The gates, when shut, have gates of their own fore and aft to protect them against vandals. The fables seem to warn against flatterers, against opportunists. Charlie is politely inattentive to my comments about the beauty and moral purpose of these gates. I am talking, I recognize, too much. But then, so is he.

Because what is this he's saying? "Mommy. Mommy. Mommy," in accents uncannily close to hers, like some mimic bird. Spoken so purely, the name seems an accusation, an indictment. Because she is not here. How could I have expected to be to him what she is—my sister, who sleepily saw us off at the apartment door, arms hunched above the bulge where Charlie's rival is waiting to be born? Ought I to return him right now?

But Charlie goes on softly saying her name, and his face is as serene as a snowman's. Lightly I buss the feathery top of his head. "Daddy, Daddy," he breathes abstractedly, stroking a polished bronze rosette. He will speak these names all through our afternoon; they become a kind of litany, a primitive om, a hum.

Charlie and I are at the gates. Then he hunkers to examine a curved leaf with burnt edges. He finds a sewer grating. He offers me a glittery arrowhead-shaped stone, and I release it through the grating; together we watch it plop onto the leaves below. A few shabby leaves still cling to their trees, and the sky is mottled with cirrus and cumulus clouds. Leaf dust and blue car exhaust eddy around us. It is a mild, smoky, parti-colored day and, now that I think of it, Halloween.

We enter the playground where a girl died walking her dogs, shot by a sniper in full sight of the nurses and mothers and little children. The playground is empty today. Charlie marches straight ahead. Receding, he dwindles to the size of a red-and-blue doll soldier. He is not at all fazed by the huge slides and swings, the seesaw that looks as if it were meant for giant children with big red hands and ears. Solemnly he makes the circuit of these enormous toys, then slides over to the sandbox, which is the only thing the playground contains that is the right size for him. Charlie crouches on the brown-sugar sand, singing tonelessly, "Teetaw Margie Daw—"

And the playground quickens with those other inhabitants of Charlie's world, Jack and Margery and Wee Willie Winkie, the ones who dwell in that crazy, funny, disturbing place innocent of the principles of physics or biology, where dogs laugh, frogs go courting, and children suffer outrageous accidents—fall down or are beaten—while the gingerbread man runs triumphantly, thumbing his nose at the farmer's wife. I try to sing along, but

Seesaw, Margery Daw,
Sold her bed and lay upon straw

are the words that come to mind. I cannot remember Charlie's version of the song. Some grownups remember better than others. Robert despised memories, though he did claim that his mistrust of a certain relative dated from some early Christmas when she sent him a sinister greeting card, depicting the old man who requests you please to put a penny in his hat—and that may be true, because I do not recall that he ever gave anything to a beggar.

With a blue tin shovel, Charlie pats the sand into heaps. "Row row row," he sings (it is his bathtub song). He sighs. "Mommy. Daddy," he says, climbing out of the sandbox. He takes my hand and we go up a stone ramp with the stroller to the top of the hill that overlooks the playground, with its outcropping of rock, the bone of Manhattan. On the grass a group of young people sprawl indolently in a circle while a large golden dog cavorts around them. Their musical instruments lie in a heap. They seem like a company of troubadours (or beggars), brightly dressed and riding high. They smell of incense. Charlie looks not at them but at a small boy who runs on tiptoes across the grass, grandparental protest screaming after him: "William! No. No. No."

A breathless grandmother tags him at last, carries him, with a jangle of bracelets, over to where we have parked the stroller, watching. The grandfather, who wears a red beret, comes along at a more sedate speed. "He's got the dickens in him today, all right," Grandmother boasts, fanning herself with a handkerchief.

William prepares to take off again, like the gingerbread man, and the grandfather makes a church out of his joined fingers to distract him. "How old is he?" I inquire, instantly jealous for Charlie of William's superior size and energy. It turns out that they are exactly the same age.

If William is sturdier, Charlie is handsomer. He is a conventionally stunning child, with the blank blond beauty of the very young, but nevertheless such as Raphael might have painted. Today the warmth and wind have lit him, set red circles on his cheeks, made a nimbus of his yellow hair. The blondness, of course, is temporary, and already fading. Still, I do not believe that either my sister or I resembled him at any moment of our lives. "I'm only his aunt," I apologize.

William is swinging an orange papier-mâché basket with a face painted on it; Charlie still has the blue tin shovel. They look at each other. We three custodians allow them to swap. "That's a pumpkin, baby," I explain to my nephew; he echoes, "Pump'n." The grandchild bangs the borrowed shovel against a wooden fence.

"Hiah, *dog*," says Charlie, drifting over to where the teen-agers preserve their circle. Dog leans on his forepaws and woofs softly. A long pink tongue swipes Charlie's face; frowning, he backs away, accompanied by cracked, adolescent laughter. His face crumples, but he does not cry. Quickly I go to him and we stroll out onto the rocks. With papery fingernails Charlie scrapes at a particle of mica, crooning his names. He has left the funny-face basket some way behind him.

It would be pleasant to linger here, but I was urged to *wear him out*, so, feeling almost professional now, I collect Charlie, pumpkin basket, tin shovel, stroller, and Charlie (he has caught some of the dickens from William); returning the basket, we bid farewell to the grandparents and cross the street of cyclists, whom Charlie greets with a friendly "Hiah, *bike*."

We are on a rustic path under tall oaks and sycamores, half-leaved, a tapestry forest. The shadows deepen and there seems to be nobody around. We come to the edge of a cliff. We look down. The canyon below us is a habitat for every species and race of vehicle: blue cars, Buick cars, convertibles, taxi cars, police cars, buses, motorcycles, hurrying east. They sound like the sea. I hold firmly to the dangling hood of Charlie's jacket while Charlie fiercely and obsessively identifies the vehicles in their flight, as though he were necessary to them; he could not stop even if he wanted to. " 'N a car. 'N a tackie car. 'N a bus." Green car, taxi car, taxi car, motorcycle. The time of warblers is long past, and Robert and I will never again eat cheese and drink beer and quarrel in the Ramble. (Once he asked, "Can't you say anything *right?*" and burst into tears, hiding his face in his hands.) The Park belongs to Charlie. I cover his red sneakers with leaves. He shifts and leans against my knee.

My ears ring with the beginnings of nursery rhymes: "How many miles to Babylon?" "There was an old woman lived under a hill." "Bobby Shaftoe's gone to sea." "I run and I run as fast as I can." *You can't catch me*, says the gingerbread man. It is Halloween. The Park begins to rustle with presences. Look, one of them is over there, a man in a leaf-green cap slouched against a maple tree, watching us. Well, he is watching us, but he is doing something else, too. Where did he come from? What is he doing? What is *that* in his *hand?*

In a single movement, I pop Charlie into the stroller, wheel it around, and get us back down the leafy path to the bikes and the people. Charlie has noticed nothing wrong! I have performed a responsible act, for a change. I am not even shaking. Best of all, Charlie does not mind relinquishing the cars. Perhaps he enjoys my company.

However, he does not care for being in the stroller, squirms in the seat, wants to walk like a man. To live. As we go up the sidewalk, Charlie, voluble now, greets everybody who passes, every animate thing. "Hiah, man!" he shouts expansively. "Hiah, girl." A gray squirrel glares at us from behind a litter basket, and he murmurs, "Hiah, kirl."

It is getting dark; a policeman rides up to us on a dappled horse. ("*Hi*ah, horsie.") "It's getting dark, lady, and the Park isn't so safe," he warns us gravely. I thank him, and we walk on.

* * * * *

At the top of the rise, the trees give way to a vast open space, a field that seemingly extends to the horizon, the jagged wall of city. The field looks emerald in the late-afternoon light. Purple and black clouds are blowing across a Walpurgisnacht sky, with the new moon suspended in it like a jack-o'-lantern smile. Near the road is a goal cage with scuffed earth around it, but no one is keeping it. Not far from it a real pumpkin glows warmly on the grass. Whoever put it there is not in view. Charlie runs to it as if recognizing an old friend. "Pump'n. Pump'n!"

With a deliberately silly smile, he tugs at its curved green handle, but the pumpkin only rolls foolishly about its axis and will not be budged. Beside the pumpkin, surrealistically juxtaposed, is a pair of oxblood-colored loafers, approximately size 10. I have the sense that

Peter's wife is going to peek out of the pumpkin, or a troop of tiny children file into a shoe. I look around for a barefoot pumpkin owner. However, nothing here is in the least strange to Charlie. One sneakered foot slides into one of the loafers, then the other into the other. Trying to navigate, he falls over backward. "Daddy," he says. He capers away on light feet and looks at the pumpkin lovingly. "Look at the *moon*, baby," I tell him. It is almost too much for him.

Charlie lifts his hands toward the moon and revolves in a dance of admiration, conducting some ceremony of his own. The Park gathers itself and freezes. For a beat in time, wind, noise, wheels are stilled. The animals in the Zoo are listening. The gingerbread man stops running. I feel as though all my life I have been traveling toward this spot, to wait beside this baby at the vortex of his joy. In the spooky silvery light, everything is a clue. There are clues all around me, but I cannot interpret them. I cannot even distinguish the mystery.

Then a cloud is dragged across the moon, a boy comes along with a loud transistor radio, bats emerge and begin to tumble in the violent air. It is at last time to go. But something else unexpected develops— Charlie does not want to leave the shoes behind. We were so happy for a while, I cannot bear that anything should change it. I carry him under the armpits over to the stroller, but he runs disconsolately away, back to the objects of his fixation. "Daddy." He is trying to tell me something. He cannot make me understand. Somehow he manages to lift one shoe by the heel, trundling it back to me, like a mother cat dragging a large brown kitten. His anxiety makes me hurt too. "Oh, Charlie," I tell him, "I *wish* we could take the shoes. But they don't belong to us. Somebody needs them, somebody with cold feet." But nobody appears to claim them.

Then it comes to me with the simplicity of faith that 10 is not an uncommon size, and all he is trying to tell me is that he thinks these are the shoes of his father. Under this light, with the air full of distant flighty things, it is a supposition too reasonable to dispute.

However, I think I now know where we are and what to say. "Going home, Charlie. Wave bye-bye shoes. Bye-bye pumpkin." We wave farewell to the moon, to the Park and all its kind and dangerous inhabitants. On the sidewalks outside the Park, the first small pirates and witches and Batmen will already be out begging; next year Charlie will be among them. I wish there were more that I could do for him.

Did I ever care so much for another person that even his clothes were holy to me?

I am thirty years old and I have no child and no attachments. If Robert came to me barefoot across the meadow I would turn my back on him, having mastered the knowledge that you can love someone and not be able to live with him, and that there are no grownups who can tell you what to do.

A Touch of Nature

THE HEALY CHILDREN ARE BURYING A CARDINAL. It died, we fear, of pollution. They found it this morning on its back by the garage, stiff as a stuffed bird, shrimp feet pointed at the sky. Now it lies like a red clown in a Kleenex box that has been lined with aluminum foil scalloped at the edges. Its beak is as shiny as nail polish. Tommy Healy touches the wing feathers gently. "You're supposed to close their eyes before you bury them. But you can't with birds because their eyelids are different, sort of double."

Tommy is eleven, and already something of a naturalist. His eyes are blue as the nearby Sound, heavily fringed and enormous. His two sisters look at the bird with eyes just like his, though the effect is not quite so startling. "Poor birdie," sighs the six-year-old. The nine-year-old tells me, "We imagine probably it was something he ate."

"Birdie, birdie," sings something from the arborvitae tree. The cardinal's widow? We hope not. Tommy puts a lid on the coffin, and sets the box in the hole they've dug. The Healy graveyard is filling up.

Though there is legwork, with neighborhood children acting as scouts, I really don't know where they get so many dead animals. Pollution, certainly, has been a help. Only last week an oil slick was reported on the Premium River, that suburban backwater. They found a bird, perhaps a sandpiper, whose feathers were matted with oil. "It looked as though it had been tarred and feathered," Tommy said.

Still, the mortality rate among Healy pets is suspiciously high.

Now Tommy shovels dirt over the box and fills in the hole; the sisters sprinkle in a few clods. "We sometimes say a little prayer," he says, "but my mother thinks that's blasphemous. But one of us pronounces a eulogy. Let's see—" He closes his eyes. "Here is a bird who died in his prime, before his usefulness was ended. None of us knew him in life, but we mourn him in death. He gave us beauty with his feathers and his song. Farewell, beautiful cardinal." The speech has a practiced ring to it. Nevertheless, it is a creditable, even moving, effort.

Having eulogized the corpse, Tommy and his sisters briskly complete the interment. There are no tears in the Healy eyes. They edge the neat mound with pebbles, cover it with maple leaves, and finally decorate it with a cross fashioned from Good Humor sticks. With a medium soft pencil Tommy inscribes it, "Cardinal. 19??—July 7, 1971."

We leave the cool maple shadows at the edge of the Healy property, where it borders on my father's. He is working in his rose garden, and gives them a Crimson Glory for the grave. With some amusement he tells me that the children applied for permission to extend the brick-bordered plot beyond the Healy property line, but he had to put the kibosh on that. "Eventually I wouldn't have room for my mulch pile."

In the unlikeliest ways, the land is threatened.

* * * * *

Two other children tended such a graveyard once, the summer the war ended. It was in New Hampshire, in a tamarack grove behind their rented summer cottage. (The tamarack, or larch, said their father, is the only coniferous tree that sheds its needles in autumn.) They were sisters, four and six; the littler one had curly hair and still wet her bed, while the older wore braids and was slightly less foolish. Both were constantly coming down with minor respiratory infections and cried a lot, which was one reason they were taken to the country, "For the Children's Sake" being one of the vaguely sinister adult phrases to which their ears were attuned. "Am I a Problem Child, Mommy?" asked the younger, one night as she was picked up to be taken to the bathroom.

The other reason was the boom on summer rentals of houses close to the city. They lived then in the house that is next to the Healys', but at that time the Healys' wasn't even a glint in a subdeveloper's eye. From their nursery they looked out across a lane onto a wide field of high grass and a small abandoned orchard. They passed only six houses when they wheeled their doll prams to the beach, where most of the lifeguards had gone to war. Because of the war and the boom, and for the children's sake, the mother took the children to New Hampshire, the father moving into an apartment in town. But he visited them often in their lakeside cottage.

The suburbs were more like country then than a lot of the country is today. But they had never been away from home before. All the first night a bird sang into their lately infected ears, "Little *girls*, little *girls*, little *girls*." Their father named it for them: whippoorwill. He looked forward to naming for them many of the wonders of nature.

"If I catch that loudmouthed wonder of nature that kept me awake all last night I'm going to snatch it bald-headed," said their mother.

That last wartime summer made everybody nervous, itching for the onset of peace. On V-E Day, the older child heard all the bells in the village ring as she rode her tricycle in the garage where the Studebaker was stalled, long unused. "Now that the war is over, can I have a balloon?" she inquired later, for the war was mainly an absence of goods: balloons, chocolate, Christmas-tree ornaments, bubble gum, nylon stockings—scarce or fabulous things no longer available to consumers. The girls used red and blue cardboard ration-point disks for play money. Some evenings they helped pull down every shade in the house—blackout, a grown-up game. A cousin, Buddy, visited them when his ship came in (he never got used to the Navy, and to the end of his days in service referred to the "front" and "back" of a ship). Cora, the cook, who squeezed roses onto their birthday cakes, went to work at a parachute factory and died of pneumonia. One afternoon, the older child got up from her nap early and witnessed a platoon of soldiers marching up Hazel Lane with guns and khaki helmets—an epiphany apparently granted only to her. They said she dreamed it.

The day after the church bells, she had a dream of dying. Taken to the hospital in a taxi (because of gas rationing), she was placed on an operating table to have her tonsils cut out. "Breathe into the balloon," bade the doctors; she did, and saw the world. It was blue and green and round like the globe in the library and got smaller and smaller as she soared away from it, till she was scared it would vanish altogether.

In the country, thin, tearful, normally unwell, the little girls throve like mushrooms. "Do you remember how the dogs used to mess under the table?" reminisced their mother once. No, they did not remember that, they remembered the food in the communal dining room at the Big House, a sprawling New England added-on farmhouse facing the small lake, exotic things unencountered in the suburbs—scalloped puffballs from the woods, toasted bacon rinds, fresh eggs every morning and real maple syrup instead of Karo, frogs' legs that they saw kicking in the kitchen sink detached from their frogs. The sink was full of green cutworms the frogs had eaten, which had once fed on the tomatoes they had in their salad that night. It was a lesson in ecology. Their father encouraged them to sample everything. At first they ate mainly for the love of him.

There were other children at Wilbur Pond: Mimi and Kit from Larchmont, their cousins Dave and Mikey and the baby, Grace from the farm and her myopic little brother, and a pack of loud boys who stuck together and played at war—*banzai!* in the meadow grass. They all swam in the lake in the daytime and came together evenings on the dewy turf outside the woodbine-twisted veranda of the main house for games of running and hiding. Ardently they chased fireflies to store their flickering radiance in mayonnaise jars with holes punched in the lids; in the morning all but one would have died, a pale-gray bug without light in a jar that smelled like old tea.

The mothers spent a lot of time sitting on the veranda chatting, writing letters. Mrs. Mimi-and-Kit tried to interest the women in nature walks in the woods, but usually ended up, an amiable patsy, picking mushrooms with the children on her own. The woods were pungent, surprising, lively. After a shower, efts appeared on the paths, soft sprites the length of a little finger with tiny red buttons down the back, not always distinguishable from the soil but in the hand bright as blood. Aside from their color they seemed totally without defenses. The children were discouraged from collecting them, especially after one of them said, "Here, Mom, could you hold this a minute?" and popped a velvety eft right into Mom's automatically extended palm.

There were tree toads on the bark, sometimes no bigger than the warts they resembled. And, everywhere, mushrooms—orange, red, amethyst, white, shaped like shells or coral or sponges or umbrellas ("Do you realize that's *poison*, an amanita?" said their father, throwing out a bunch that had dissolved into black mush in a corner of their bedroom).

But he showed them something else, tiptoeing with them out into the noisy night—a sea-green moth stuck against a window screen, feathered white as foam and with spots like owl eyes on its forewings. The Luna moth. *Actias luna.* He killed it with lighter fluid and mounted it for them on a piece of cardboard; it was the start of a moth collection. (The Luna and other moths repose in their shadow box somewhere in the attic still, their color diminished but not yet overcome.)

One sister stood in the field alongside their cottage, a crescent of grass and weeds backed by woods. A garden spider had spun its wiry web into the crotch of an old fruit tree—*Argiope aurantia*, a fat black-and-gold horror. At the base of the tree, hardly trembling, lay an immature rabbit badly torn by the mess-table dogs or other animals. Insects hummed in the grass amid foamy nets of grasshopper spit. But the day seemed scarcely to breathe. She gathered the rabbit, without looking, into the hem of her pinafore and ran to her parents, beginning to cry for its blood and pain. It had been laid open on its right side like an anatomical drawing, down to muscle and bone.

"Oh my God, put it out of its misery," their mother said. They put it instead in a carton and ministered to it with lettuce, and water in a jar top. In the morning its eyes were open but it had stopped trembling for good.

Their mother said it was hopping in rabbit heaven.

Their father made it a coffin out of a bracelet box (it was so tiny), and donated a handkerchief for a shroud. The girls remembered a place, a clearing—the grownups had to bend and tear their way there on a path their father supposed had been made by deer. He dug a hole with a wooden toy shovel they had brought from the suburbs.

Are all funerals the same? Like the Healys, these children knelt, sprinkled dirt over the coffin, and filled in the hole. "Say goodbye," their father told them. Then they all closed their eyes and reflected on rabbit heaven. The children picked field flowers for the grave until it was time for lunch.

Soon the other sister came home, gagging, with a toad that had been run over by the milk truck. The sisters edged the two graves with pebbles and revealed the place to the rest of the children.

Mrs. Mimi-and-Kit discovered, under some toys in Kit's room, a dead starling dripping maggots. Even before pollution, there was no shortage of dead animals in New Hampshire.

The clearing became a cemetery, a garden of moss, bark, and drooping wild flowers. After a wet spell, boletus mushrooms gilded the roots of the larches, and Indian pipes abounded, ghastly mourners. Peaceful and bored on late afternoons, the proprietors of the graveyard dug into the friable soil to inter whatever mammal, reptile, amphibian, or bird had fallen by the wayside. The other children helped, but it belonged to them.

On the veranda, the mothers talked. Mr. Wilbur, the creased-faced Yankee who ran the place, made a killing on the black market, which was to the children an imagined, torchlighted cavern in the hills piled with heaps of rubber tires, mountains of candy, tubs of butter, festoons of balloons. Hiroshima, the war will soon be over. Grace Prenty was more closely related to her uncle than she should be, whisper. Nagasaki.

The Prentys ran, in their fashion, the farm up the hill from the Wilbur property. That was where the eggs and milk came from. And the cows, who pastured on Wilbur land, near the cottages—they were restless and prone to nocturnal rampages. One night they surrounded the cottages like thunder, and the girls quivered in their beds, thinking the house would collapse. Every evening at five, Trantus Prenty, with a lot of switching and cursing, herded them uphill to the Prenty milking barn, dogs snapping at their hoofs. The cows were in no hurry to get back to their quarters, which held an ammoniac reek that brought tears to the eyes.

Often the little girls followed the cows to the milking, with the other children. Their father could milk a cow; he could squirt a stream of milk dexterously into the pail, or the mouth of a barn cat or a child's. It steamed in the bucket, a foamy broth that tasted like condensed—not much like what they drank later in the dining room; one warm taste sufficed.

The Prentys were an iron-age family, their farm a barnyard zoo like a picture-book illustration, only real with flies and barn smells. Four generations of women lived there—all of them, including nearly nubile, twelve-year-old Grace, missing their upper front teeth. Whenever one outbuilding was filled with animals or tools, the Prentys threw up another that seemed to be supported by sheer luck. They turned the soil with plows drawn by weary wind-broken thirty-year-old horses. They are probably plowing that way now. The summer people were enchanted.

Reciprocating their interest, Grace visited the Wilbur place with her little brother when she wasn't busy with farm chores. Her mother a drudge, her putative father the town arsonist, she lisped incomprehensibly sometimes—a case history of inbreeding and malnutrition, her destiny manifest. But she was gentle with the Prenty animals, helpful and indulgent with young things, and the mothers liked having her around.

Grace was full of stories. She told the sisters that babies came out of your belly button and that if you spit in a church you would go blind. They showed her the graveyard with its flowers and mossy mounds. "It's like a picture," she observed wistfully. She showed them how to make dandelion wreaths and grass whistles.

When she couldn't come down, the sisters visited the Prenty place. Sometimes she let them help her feed the animals. There were chickens in the back yard, rabbits in the cellar, pigs rooting near the privy, goats around the porch, and broody hens in the abandoned truck bodies near the woods. They played with the offspring of the fecund barn cats and came home with fleabites sprinkled over their skinny legs. Their mother thought they had developed a summer allergy.

Grace's brother Andy, who was six or seven but looked younger, was something different; nature had issued him a reprieve (or perhaps an outside set of genes). The other Prentys were milk-pale, straw-haired, exophthalmic. He seemed a changeling, a gypsy child with a mop of black hair through which pointy ears protruded alertly, and deep, blinking eyes. He was thin, probably wormy, a sad little boy who didn't take up much room.

He hardly ever spoke, but he used his eyes and ears. The little girls' mother used to read to them on the porch after lunch, as a substitute for the naps that they had outgrown. Though she read to *them*, the other children came and listened, too, collapsed in various postures around the rocker where she sat. She read well, in a rich, interesting voice. The book was *The Wind in the Willows*.

"'. . . with his ear to the reed-stems he caught, at intervals, something of what the wind went whispering so constantly among them,'" she read, and closed the book over one thumb. They were sleepy, belly-full, semi-attentive. "Do you like this book? Would you rather have another one?" Sailboats skimmed like waterbugs on the glaring surface of the pond. A daddy longlegs with its ridiculously graceful limbs climbed up a pillar and down again. Yes, they liked it. Now probably they could go swimming.

But Andy lingered, with such a fasting look she asked if he wanted to see the pictures.

Nobody in Andy's house had ever read a book to him. But Andy, it turned out, could read. So she let him read the books they had brought from the nursery, crouching gnomishly in the shadows by the steps of their cottage. He read about a horse who pulled a vegetable wagon in New York City and pined for the country. When the horse's dream came true because of automation, he mourned, recognizing that he was a city horse after all. It had a happy ending; the master came and took him back to the city. Andy read almost everything they had. He adopted their books, and nobody bothered him by asking him to play, or warned him that reading in the dark would hurt his eyes.

It was a busy summer. The children kept a collective zoo at Mrs. Mimi-and-Kit's; its main feature was a terrarium full of mean, energetic garter snakes that could get through the least cracks. Despite the ban on efts, the red things were ubiquitous. Some ended in the graveyard, others in bureau drawers. The efts, explained their father, were the terrestrial cycle of the red-spotted newt, or salamander, a water creature. In time their bodies would darken and alter and they would return to live out their lives in the water.

"Oh, I think I see one changing," said the younger girl, bending over a bright spot on the path.

Despite the sisters' teaching, they could not get Grace to dog-paddle in the shallow lake; she sank immediately and repeatedly to the bottom, even in a foot of water. She was bored by the zoo and the moth collection. The funerals, however, inspired her. She whispered to the animals as they put them in the ground, like some straw-maned country sorceress. She found a star-nosed mole for them to bury. And, of course, the Prenty farm provided an abundance of funeral fodder.

The evening she showed up with a deceased piglet, even the children blanched. "Good God, it's a dead baby," muttered a parent. Grace had raised it on a bottle. They buried it wrapped in a pillowcase.

* * * * *

Tommy and his sisters are taking turns swinging from the rope my father hung from the apple tree for the grandchildren. Waiting his turn, Tommy tells me there have been vandals in the graveyard. Somebody has dug up several animals and absconded with their bodies, including that of a pet kitten. "We're pretty sure we know who it is," he says. "We haven't caught him, but we've put a tail on him."

It will be grim for that young resurrectionist.

Yes, in the woods were vandals, too, foxes or porcupines or dogs, who scrabbled up the mold and left a shambles the children had to spend a morning clearing up. At least one of them wept over the devastation. But the fungi and Indian pipes, the saprophytes sprouted even more abundantly, as though nourished by the material with which the children had enriched the wilderness.

* * * * *

Every time their father came up, he brought them presents. One week it was a packet of little colored-paper flags of the nations, to be pasted on toothpick staffs. "For a rainy day," he suggested. There were not many rainy days that August. They pasted the flags onto their staffs on V-J Day, which came after Hiroshima and Nagasaki—the flags made a centerpiece for the table at dinner. Peace, peace was in the air like the wind in the willows. The room was filled with communicated joy. The soldiers were coming home. Buddy would come back unharmed. Maybe even Cora would return. There would be balloons, cheap candy, toys, Christmas ornaments, automobile rides, all the provender of peace. (A year later, the moratorium on building houses ended and the builders moved into the suburb with bulldozers, demolishing the vacant lots where the sisters had played and picked flowers to sell door-to-door, changing the view of the Sound, giving the children instead half-finished houses good for hide-and-seek where they molded things out of wet cement and collected pieces of wire and coin-shaped bits of metal for play money, setting the Healys' house and several others atop the tennis courts, burying the lily-of-the-valley patch and the rhododendron cave.) It has been a long time since anybody celebrated the end of a war like that. I am glad they had flags for the occasion.

One of the banzai boys stepped on a rusty nail at the Prentys' barn and had to be rushed to town by Mr. Wilbur for a tetanus shot. Grace said she once knew a little girl named Martha who had got lockjaw. "They had to bury her in a round coffin." The sisters were keyed up with the end of the war and the impending departure. Their father stayed with them for two weeks straight.

Long since, the whippoorwill had stopped calling them little girls and the fireflies disappeared in the grass. Because the younger girl no longer had to be picked up at night they promised to reward her with the present of a canary bird, and forgot it. Neither child had more than a passing respiratory infection all summer. After they left, Andy died of a burst appendix (the Prentys, naturally, dosed him with castor oil). "That poor little boy," recalled their mother, looking up from a letter. "He certainly liked to read."

Time for last things, to release the snakes, to make ceremonial pilgrimages to the pond and the woods. Their mother slew a hornet with a broom, and they couldn't decide whether to throw it out or mount it.

"Seven of them could kill a horse," said Grace to the sisters. They were at the Prentys', tossing handfuls of grain to the poultry. One small chick had something stuck in its craw and couldn't swallow, though it persisted in making the attempt, bobbing, pecking, and gasping; when they tried to catch it, it scurried under the house. Grace said it would not live. But it took its time perishing, and that night they caught a glimpse of its puny head, still weakly pecking and bobbing near a post, when they followed the cows to the milking barn.

The morning of the day they left, the two sisters ran out to the last things and collected some salamanders on the way—part of their scheme to stock the suburbs with red-spotted newts, beginning in their back yard. It had rained in the night; easily they picked up half a pailful. Their parents were still struggling with books, clothes, toys. "Don't go far," somebody shouted. The girls deposited their crimson surprise on the back seat of the Studebaker. The family wouldn't be ready to leave for a while; they had time.

Giggling, they started to run hand in hand up the hill to the farm, past roadside herbs their father had named for them, grown higher than they—joe-pye weed, meadowsweet, milkweed with its sweet purple heads almost finished, chicory infested with butterflies exactly the same blue.

There, by the kitchen steps, sat Andy solemnly writing in the dirt with a stick. "We have to leave," they explained. "Where's Grace?" He didn't answer, but then he often didn't. Grace, hearing their excitement, came out of the kitchen, banging the door in a hurry on a cloud of end-of-summer flies. She understood why they had come.

The chicken had wandered since they last saw it—not far; Grace found it for them a little way under the house, resting on its beak, tail up, immobile. Certainly, it was no longer hungry. It took them only a second to decide to run down and give it a proper burial.

The sisters had a coffin ready just in case—the flag box. Their parents were busy inside the cottage. They were the last family to go home, so there were only those children to kneel in the darkness of the trees, at the final grave.

Did *all* of them hear how their corpse scratched hungrily against the cardboard sides of its coffin as the first dirt fell upon the top, revived by the newness of its surroundings, or perhaps a sound like rain? Whoever of them heard, not one acknowledged it. Honk, honk snuffed the nuthatches in the branches, and the Indian pipes bent their white heads. The three children pressed hands together. Grace, with closed eyes and half-open mouth, looked truly like a halfwit.

Into the woods came the sound of parents calling.

The salamanders had easily squirmed out of the bucket and into the baggage, springs, upholstery, appearing in odd places all the way to Westchester. Still, the scolding, for the first few miles, helped drown out the whisper of those claws.

Well, it recurs from time to time, that fretful, terrible stirring, the persistence of even the weakest to go on living in the worst of circumstances. And sometimes I see, blinking in the shadows, a bony, doomed little boy they might have loved, left without a thing to read.

DAY OLD BABY RATS

DOWN NEAR THE RIVER A DOOR SLAMS; somebody wakes up, immediately flips over onto her back. She dreamed she went fishing, which is odd because she's never fished in her life. She thought someone was calling her "baby."

There's a lot of January light crawling from beneath room-darkener shades, casting mobile shadows on walls and ceiling. The mobile is composed of hundreds of white plastic circles the size of Communion wafers. As they spin they wax and wane, swell and vanish like little moons. Their shadows are like summer, like leaves, the leaves of the plane tree at the window, which hasn't any, right now, being in hibernation.

Through the crack between window and sill, air that tomorrow's papers will designate Unsatisfactory flows over one exposed arm, making the hairs stand up like sentries. Long trailer trucks continue to grind along the one-way street, tag end of a procession that began at 4 a.m. with the clank and whistle of trains on dead-end sidings, as melancholy as though they were the victims they had carried across the Hudson. The trucks carry meat for the Village butcher shops, the city's restaurants—pink sides of prime beef that you cannot purchase at the supermarket, U.S.D.A. choice or commercial, pigs, lambs, chickens, rabbits, helped off the trucks by shivering men who warm their hands over trash-basket fires.

In the apartment across the hall the baby is bawling, "I want my milk."

It's cold and bloody in the refrigerated warehouses where the meat is stored prior to distribution. It's pretty cold in here, too. On her feet now, naked, she looks under the shade, which snaps smartly to the top of the window, disclosing a day: very clear for January. And colorful: stained-glass sky over a row of nineteenth-century houses painted pink and lime and lilac and beige, topped by clusters of chimney stacks, one of which emits a tornado of oily black smoke, fast dispersing. She ought to report it.

"I am sorry. The Office of Air Resources is closed till Monday. Please state the nature of the offense and the name and address of the violator and we will take action upon it when the office is open. This is a recording."

A pair of eyes on the fire escape, the golden gaze of the fat seven-toed tom from the next apartment; she hasn't a stitch on, backs away. Next thing, she's in the middle of the kitchen, bare and green as a guppy, trembling from head to toe, so much that it is difficult to open the door to the lower cabinet, which turns out to house a sizable bottle collection. On her knees she pours into a glass an ounce of scotch, part of which sloshes over the linoleum in an amber puddle, fast dispersing. She gets the glass between her teeth. One, two, three, wait—the tremor peaks, subsides. She yawns and wipes the sleep from her eyes.

Getting dressed now, the radio going, the listener-sponsored radio. Don't speak his name. He is everywhere, like spring. His eyes are leaves.

She can find only one shoe and digs desperately in the welter of foot-wear like a retreat of mercenaries in the bottom of the closet; how did she get so many shoes? She tends to lose things that go in pairs. "Where's my other glove? My new earring—who took it?" she will wonder helplessly, too old to pray to St. Anthony, patron of lost objects.

His eyes are leaves, the birds his messengers.

Certainly somebody took her wallet last week while she was shopping for pants on Eighth Street. It *was* lifted, rather than absentmindedly abandoned in a restaurant, or on top of a cigarette machine. Later that evening a thin, limping man showed up on the doorstep with one half of her driver's license. He explained he had found it in a litter basket in Washington Square.

Look, flickering in the thicket, at the heart of the thorn tree. Cold as wind—Half shod, she switches to an all-news program: It is after ten o'clock; utilities are unchanged. The other shoe is in the bathroom; she spies it—spitting out a mouthful of toothpaste—under the radiator.

The shadow of a black man, the ripple of a war.

She wraps herself in a white rabbit-fur coat and goes out without locking the door, fumbling for her huge polarized sunglasses in her leather shoulder pouch, down two flights of stairs and onto the sidewalk. Now, here is the big brown United Parcel Service truck lumbering illegally up onto the curb and halting just short of the plane tree, which bears two deep gouges where the same truck wounded it last Monday morning. The driver hustles out and starts up the steps with a brown parcel, whistling.

In the vestibule he rings her bell, which of course nobody answers, since the apartment occupant is beside the truck, copying the license plate and other relevant numbers into a little spiral notebook.

Still whistling, the young man with the brown uniform and small brown mustache comes back out with his parcel. The woman in the furry coat leans against the tree, glaring through her dark lenses.

"Lady." He stops in mid-trill. "Be nice. I can't go through this again. Just sign the little slip, I give you the package, and everybody's happy."

Through clenched teeth she says, "This time I am really going to report you. Really. Do you know that tree cost one hundred dollars to plant? And people like you, people like you—" But the last words emerge with difficulty, and tears fuzz the sharp outlines, her polarized vision of the sunny world. He cannot see the tears.

She's dying to know what is in the package. With rage the driver throws it back into the truck, THIS SIDE UP down. "You're bad news, lady," he yells, hurtling into the driver's seat; revs the motor. Afraid he's going to take out his temper on the tree, she gets in front of it, and now he cannot move the truck. "If you Don't. Get. Out. Of my. Way. I'm. Going. To Run. You. Down." His voice changes. "What do you want from me, lady?" he implores, unanswerably.

He gets his truck away without a mishap after all.

On the next block the drunk man starts out of the doorway where he has lain all night, stumbling toward her, clawing at his stained clothes. "Hey, don't I know you from somewheres?" His eyes look like pebbles, yellow and veined. "I know you. I know you a nice lady. Won'tcha gimme something, please? Fourteen cents, all I need's like fourteen cents." Smiling brilliantly, dancing around her: "I know you, I watches you comings and you goings."

Finally she digs up from the depths of her pocketbook some change, which falls to the sidewalk; he goes after it, fumbling and muttering in the gutter. All fall he was a worry to her, sleeping so still in his doorway, a crumpled overcoat, and a bottle still in its paper bag at his head like a candle. He has lost the overcoat but acquired some mittens. How does he know her? How has he managed to fight the cold this long, into January?

* * * * *

Back in the apartment with the newspapers and their interesting headlines:

4 CHAIN-STORES
FIRE-BOMBED

7 L.I. CHILDREN
DIE IN BUS CRASH

FEAR TEN SLAIN
IN RACKETS WAR

GRAVEDIGGERS
CALL STRIKE

Drug Girl, 12, Tells of Freakout

A HUNGRY BABY
DIES: JAIL MOM

*Army Dismisses Charge of
War Crimes by General*

FOE ATTACKS . . .

POPE BLESSES . . .

*Actual Tests Used to Perpare
Pupils for Reading Exams*

At the table, with a cup of tea and a cigarette, she gets the gist of the day's news and what the department stores are featuring, since she has errands to run, things to buy. Fidgeting, tongue between her teeth. ("Don't *do* that," her mother used to say watchfully, "you'll ruin your occlusion." Reaching the weather report (occluded front), she looks warily around, as though she were being watched. But there is nobody in the house, which is suddenly so quiet the only sound is her own, her heartbeat.

There are no clocks in the apartment. What time has it gotten to be? She rushes to the telephone to dial the time, and when she lifts the receiver a voice is immediately in her ear. "Washington operator here. I have a person-to-person call for Mmm. Blur. Hello, New York, will you accept the call, please, New York?" Superimposed on the operator's voice is another, tinny and distant—a woman's?—but she cannot make out the words.

Who does she know in Washington?

No, she will not accept the call, she will not accept the charges. It must be past noon; the sun will be setting before too long. Before 4:37, according to the newspaper.

She has not lost her wristwatch, but she cannot seem to extricate it from the repair shop; it's been there for three weeks with a shattered crystal and a broken hand that she suspects they're keeping in traction. She turns her own hands palms up; the creases gleam with sweat—snail tracks.

Steadier now, tongue emergent, she's refilling a pocket flask from the kitchen liquor supply. It's a four-ounce hip-hugger model with a cute red leather jacket that can be unbuttoned for cleaning; she carries it everywhere in case of emergency, of entrapment in subway or elevator. Its predecessor fell on the floor of the ladies' room at the Art Students League, where she was waiting for a perennial art student to finish his life-studies class so they could go out to dinner and drinks or vice versa; how sorry she was to lose it! But she quickly replaced it with an identical model from Hoffritz.

With him she went to an island remote from the city and from everything else. Ten miles out in the Atlantic, off the coast of Maine, where the foghorn cries all night long, once a minute, "It *hurts,*" warning ships off the rocks where lobsters lie low (skittering anyway into the baited traps) and the brightest thing by night is the eye of the lighthouse, since the island is without community electricity. The wind blew constantly on the headlands several hundred feet over the sea. When the fog lifted, the ocean was the color of melted blue wax. Way down on the rocks, seals grazed, polychromatic as pigeons: blue, gray, brown, and spotted. Once, they thought they saw far out the spout of a whale.

Some sportsmen that week harpooned a small whale, a blackfish, and towed it into the harbor, stranding it on Fish Beach. All afternoon they worked to extract their three spearheads, up to the armpits in blubber, till the sand was red and sticky and thick with flies.

She and he walked in the woods, when he wasn't painting, watched birds and the sunset, ate lobster with slippery fingers. Then she had an appetite, and used to collect leftover oranges or bananas from other tables to devour thoughtfully at night while the lighthouse spun and the foghorn ached. Having gone through her fruit and her library books, she got into bed at last; he sighed, set on by his own bad dreams. It wasn't a success, that holiday. Making love in a blueberry patch, they reached up for berries and ate them where they lay. The days seemed very long. On the rocky cliffs they fought, wind whipping their barbed words out to sea. Back on the mainland, at the bus terminal, early in the morning: "You'll be all right?" he asked, peering into her face as though it were a steamed-up mirror.

On the river, a ship leaving for Valparaiso when the shipping page said it would sounds its plangent departure whistle—music for bones. Three times, as if it would never end, then ends for that particular voyage. It makes her eyes water.

Tropical fish in the living room move around in their tank, weaving gaudily through the underwater foliage, striped golden angelfish, jewel-like neon tetras, gouramis, a fat black molly. The one-eyed catfish oozes along the bottom of the aquarium as though vacuuming a rug. As she bends over them they rise, expecting a shower of ant eggs, frantically kissing the surface. She has forgotten to feed them. Again.

* * * * *

Somebody leaves the house for the second and final time that day. A fire siren evokes the noise of every dog on the block. There has been a fire in the Chinese laundry. An old Italian lady in a greasy black dress giggles at the snakes in the pet-shop window, her week's groceries piled in her grocery cart, and her cat on top of them. *He spreads like fire— don't smile.*

The Goodwill Exterminators have a new exhibit: among the pick-led bugs and childishly hand-lettered signs, a jar of milk-white shrimps with tails, labeled "Day-old baby Rats, caught in a Vokswagon on Perry Street by Leon." She digs her nails into her gloveless palms. *Don't smile; he hates it. Pretend not to tremble.* She checks her left wrist to see what time it is.

The sign over the bank spells out time and temperature in yellow dots:

12:57

79°

Very warm for January.

Near the subway entrance she buys the afternoon paper, and a man pushes her change over the papers with his hook.

* * * * *

The train stops just outside of the Fourteenth Street station and refuses to budge for several minutes. At Twenty-third Street, for some reason, a mob storms the cars, hustling for seats. A very small woman gets jammed in the half-open door—a midget, really, but still an ordinary-looking middle-aged woman in an out-of-style tweed coat and an out-of-town hat with a little veil, which is looped rakishly, accidentally, over one ear. She appears so helpless that somebody offers her a seat. "Hurry up, Daddy! Over here!" The other half of the door shuts, and she screams. The door opens. Her husband, who is taller, but only by an inch, rushes in, swinging a tiny child over the edge of the platform. They plop him onto the seat she gave up and stand guard, protectively.

"I need a lollipop," the baby shouts over the shriek of the train; no larger than a year-old infant, an achondroplastic dwarf without his parents' good proportions, with very short plump baby arms and no legs to speak of. His forehead bulges above a big, perplexed face, mouth turned down at the corners. Like any child he squirms petulantly in his seat, under a sign which reads "Little enough to ride for free? Little enough to ride your knee!" Daddy midget gives him a lemon lollipop.

She has to cook dinner for eight people next Thursday. She picks out a five-quart casserole in Macy's basement, tries to charge it, discovers that all her credit cards are missing, buys it anyway, orders it sent. "Jeez, Miss, didn't you inform Credit yet?" The elevator to Credit is suffocatingly hot and reeks of fur and perfume. It stops at every floor, and by the eighth she has recalled that she has no charge account with Macy's.

(The U.P.S. man will make a real effort to deliver the dish in time, nicking off more of the bark of the plane tree; ringing and ringing but nobody's home.)

Sweating in her fur coat, she proceeds down the maze that leads to the subway platform, through a crowd of people eating ice-cream cones and asking which way to the Port Authority Bus Terminal; nearly bumps into a soldier who has taken a post by a gum machine. Not an ordinary G.I. but someone on his way to a revolution. Leaf-patterned trousers tucked into combat boots, combat jacket of a different green, green beret pulled down nearly over his eyebrows—even his canteen is in camouflage. Only his gun is not. He holds his rifle butt end down between his boots like a walking stick. He stares impassively over the crowd, as though he thinks he is invisible. And perhaps he is.

She has reached the last staircase when there is a voice at her back, a whisper: "Hey lady, you need help with your packages?" But her hands are empty.

She is holding very tightly to the railing. Another voice: Middle-aged lady who inquires kindly, "Are you sick, Miss? Do you need some help!"

She shakes her head no, but the lady helps her down anyway, talking cozily. "You know, I had a friend once was so scared of the subway she'd get nauseous when the train came in. It's called claustrophobia? Well, finally the husband made her see the doctor. Well, it turned out that her brother locked her in a closet once when she was a bitty thing, and she'd forgotten all about it. But her heart remembered." A leap of the heart. "You know, it was a funny thing. After she got well and rode subways without thinking twice about it, she had one of those freak accidents and almost lost an arm on a Flushing train. I bet the operations cost her more than the psychiatrist did. Well, honey, here's your train."

Tottering onto the lit car, she supports herself against a post, breathes easier until the doors have closed and the train starts down the dark passage. With a felt-tip pen, someone has lettered on the L&M ad, "God is a Sadist."

* * * * *

Quickly tiring of her own reflection in the dressing-room mirrors, she buys the first dress she tried on, a silky blue Ban-Lon number that makes her look thin as a doll. There is a delay when she tries to charge it. Shifting from foot to foot with impatience, says yes, she will report the loss.

(She will be extremely surprised when next tenth of the month a bill arrives from this department store for $600 worth of merchandise she never purchased. But perhaps she will have notified Credit Service in time to avoid the liability.)

A very young girl with a face like an angel's sits in an armchair in the ladies' lounge, breast bare to her infant daughter; the baby nurses with an expression of concentration, pink palm closing and unclosing rhythmically like a sea anemone. The mother's knees are spread in fatigue. Assorted clothes, diapers, bottles, and magazines are falling out of the department-store shopping bags beside her chair. She looks as though she has been traveling a long time. She has just gone to sleep; eyelashes hover like black spiders over her cheekbones. She snores.

Baby loses the soda fountain and wails angrily. Her mother automatically readjusts the small head and closes her eyes upon the world once more, breathing onto it the syllables, like prayer, "Goddam son-of-a-bitch bastards."

"Breathe in," the nurse instructed. "Pant. Harder." She tried to, like a good girl, sobbing obediently. "It won't hurt so much this way." Actually, it hurt very little. "It works like a vacuum cleaner." Nature, she said, abhors a vacuum. "I usually have a cleaning woman," she told the fluorescent ceiling lights.

A sip from the red flask in the toilet, followed by a rush of acid.

Outside on Fifth Avenue, asbestos flakes eddy in spiral air currents like snow, the carcinogenic emission from the new skyscraper. Something blows into her eye before she can get out her dark glasses. She blinks to tear it away.

Bells jangle. The saffron robes, the shaven-head Hindu followers chanting "Hare Krishna" surround her, offering their literature with gentle words. Under their sleazy peach-tinted rayon saris they wear sweaters and sweatshirts, and sneakers instead of sandals. Surely they're in the wrong climate. They sing, "Hare Krishna, Hare Krishna, Krishna Krishna, Hare Hare," snapping their belled fingers and jouncing to ward off the cold.

The literature is called "Back to Godhead," and shows a circle of girls with pleated skirts like fans dancing beneath stylized Indian flowers, a round moon. "Hare Rama, Hare Rama, Rama Rama, Hare Hare," the hectic singers chant.

"Oh my God, isn't that Al Silberstang from Fire Island?" says a passer-by, nudging her companion to a halt. Al Silberstang does not cease from his dance. His eyes dwell on inner secrets. She searches for money so she can escape their circle. "Peace, peace, lady," says Al Silberstang, whirling away with her money. But there is no peace from the Hindus, no peace from the chestnut and pretzel sellers, one at each corner, warming their hands over the braziers and reiterating their spiel.

Escaping across the street, she looks up to see where she is—a mistake; her head begins to spin. What did she eat for breakfast?

Here she is, the rival sect's headquarters, St. Patrick's Cathedral. A man on the steps brandishes a sign, "ANNOYING SICK H-BOMB DICTATOR WILL BE PUNISHED," at an old lady in an old mink, in a walker, going up the steps with the aid of a younger female, daughter or niece, who looks put-upon and cold in her short cloth coat. The old lady's arm is grasped on the other side by a nun. You can tell it is a nun from the navy-blue tailored outfit, like an airline stewardess's, and the truncated veil, revealing a steel-gray curly bang. Nuns never used to have gray hair. Or calves. The nuns of her youth floated like blackbirds. Step. By step. By step, the old lady is guided through a small door set into the heavily ornamented bronze ones. Around the corner is the aftermath of a Filipino wedding, the small white bride shivering and smiling for the photographers.

The nuns with their pale faces taught them myths about eternity and how to walk in processions. " 'Tis the month of our Mother, the blessed and beautiful days," the parochial schoolchildren sang in May, carrying their sheaves of wheat down suburban sidewalks, under the magnolias. A pretty sight. Though *she'd* never really cottoned to Our Lady; she much preferred the Holy Ghost, perhaps because he was a bird.

Heaven, hell, purgatory, limbo, where little unbaptized children lived pleasantly in a garden, crawling on the green grass, and it never snowed. Purgatory was where they melted your sins away; hell was very hot. (A little boy died and a saint revived him. "Oh Mother," he cried, "I have been in such a terrible place!" She is cold. And hungry: the smell of burning chestnuts rises like incense. "Getcha hot chestnuts! Getcha pretzels!"

He scatters a handful of raw nuts over the coals, extends a bagful with a hand that is like a burnt pretzel, grins brilliantly. "I bet you hungry, pretty lady; I know you—"

* * * * *

Tugging at the door to the Cathedral, where she's never been. *He eats terror, gulps tears, and spits catastrophes.* The smell of incense, dazzling banks of red votive candles, the purple light from high stained-glass windows decorated with suffering saints. Tourists move chattily around the gloom of the nave; in the side aisles kneel the reverent few. She looks dizzily at the vaulted ceiling, light-years away. She steadies herself on a granite basin. Then, to show she's all right, dabbles holy water from the font and blesses herself like the tourists just ahead. The basin has specks floating in it and a layer of silt.

Her heart beats as though it were trying to get out. Looking for a place to sit down, she travels along an enormous aisle, toward where she sees people as at the small end of the telescope her father gave her once when she was thirteen and infatuated with science. It has been years since she was in church. And what a church! Are you supposed to cover your head these days? She has no cover, not even a handkerchief to pin to her hair.

At a side pew occupied mostly by women her knees signal *no farther*, and she slides in. Her uncovered scalp prickles dangerously. She thinks, with longing, of her flask.

As she plans about getting back down the aisle, or at least behind a stone pillar, the women begin trickling out the other side of the pew. An elbow in the ribs: it is the niece or daughter of the woman in the walker. "Miss, could you please move along, or are you asleep, dope?"

Unable to reply, she shies into the aisle, abandoning (she will remember later, in a crowded room) a brown-and-white box from Saks Fifth Avenue to the niece or the H-bomb man or St. Patrick. Or him, the god of fear. There's a convenient pillar, and—what is this?—a curtained cubicle behind a brass gate, private, hidden, a good place to take stock and think her way out, back to the right door. Sneaking a backward glance, she parts the white curtain, ducks in, groping for familiar leathery corners. Just as she has the cap off and is tilting the flask back, there is a hair-raising creak. Somebody else is only a breath away. And listening. And murmuring, through a grille, *"Ja, mein Kind?"* Fallen into the hands of the Nazis. "Yes, my child," he says impatiently.

Good heavens, somebody is answering. It is her own high parochial-school voice, her very tongue snapping out the appropriate response. "Bless me, Father, for I have sinned. It has been fifteen years since my last confession." At last she gets the bottleneck in her mouth. Alcohol is instantly absorbed through the stomach lining into the bloodstream.

At once the molecules are joined up, spreading the cheerful news.

Anticipatory silence. Perhaps he only understands German. She racks her brain—she has no wish to go spilling the secrets of her life to a stranger. First you confessed sins against the Church, then against God. She remembers a sin against the Church: "I have missed Mass."

"How many times?"

"Every time." Quick swallow. A rush of confidence. "I used God's name in vain five times. I disobeyed my parents three times. I was rude to a nun once. I slapped my little sister. I was untruthful—" Running out of sins, she adds, desperately, "I smoked marijuana."

"On how many occasions?"

"I don't remember."

He clears his throat, beginning to sound like a Viennese psychiatrist. "So, is that all that you wish to tell me?"

"Well, not quite," she stalls (once more should do the trick). Then she realizes that now there are three of them in the confessional; someone else is waiting on the other side, behind the priest, making a priest sandwich, getting restless. She shifts heavily to assert her presence—probably the niece woman who called her "dope."

"Oh no, Father," she says, tilting the flask back for another round. Not all of it reaches her mouth, there's spillage; the booth fills with the odor of alcohol in addition to that of Listerine. She is tempted to offer him a nip through the grille, for his stomach's sake. "But it's been such a long time." A weak giggle. Her time, and the jig, is up.

The Big Ear is no longer fooled. "My daughter, I suspect you are spoofing me. There are penitents waiting; you are wasting my time. Why are you here? What do you want?" No answer. "Do you want absolution? If you are in some kind of trouble, we shall discuss it in the rectory at two-forty next Wednesday. Father Kleinhardt is the name."

"Father Kleinhardt, I am frightened."

"For your penance say three Hail Marys. Now make an Act of Contrition." Switching tongues, he begins to absolve her in Latin.

"I am frightened to death, Father." But he chooses not to hear.

She begins, "O my God, I am heartily sorry," and slips out, leaving him committed to the end of his Latin prayer, noticing a sign taped to the side altar: "Father Kleinhardt: English-Deutsch." At the altar of St. Anthony a prayer is posted in mock parchment, promising the reciter forty days' indulgence. She has got away with it, she is outside, she is free.

The morning she left the northern island a young deer escaped from it, the only one of the herd imported from Boothbay Harbor who couldn't settle down but rampaged through the woods like a crazy thing and ate roses out of village gardens. After they found hoofprints on the beach, they put out salt for him in the woods. He passed her boat swimming like a small horned seal in a mainland direction; it was too late and too foggy for the lobster smacks to find him. By the time she reached the city he was fathoms deep, and the fish were grazing off his antlers. "Taxi, lady?" said a cabdriver outside the Port Authority Bus Terminal. The man drove demoniacally, hunched like a jockey over the wheel; only when they reached her apartment did she observe that it was because he couldn't straighten his back. In the full glare of the street lamp his features leaped at her: the thrust chin, the snub nose, the furrowed forehead with its huge wen, the maimed, cleft, two-fingered hoof of a congenitally deformed right hand. Smiling hilariously, he scratched at the wen. "Take it easy now, lady," he told her.

(The dead deer lies among the rocks, nibbled bare by sea worms and crustaceans, far from home; barnacles have attached themselves to his skeleton; when spring comes, a fisherman will draw up with his catch its alien skull, and think it is something new.)

Once you have seen him, he will never let you get away with anything.

* * * * *

Now it is time, definitely time, to start uptown, taking it easy and crossing with the lights. The sun has gone down, leaving a stain in the west.

At a store window she acknowledges with a slight smile her reflection: a thin woman in a white coat and big black glasses, soon to be middle-aged, puzzled because the years went so fast and the days so slowly. And, someday, old.

Killing time, she stops to light a cigarette and is nearly swept over by an energetic group of tiny children, chattering in the half-light by Central Park. There are about eight of them, fat as chickadees in their snowsuits. Isn't it late for them to be out? "I'm *cold*," complains one grumpy mite with thick glasses and a circle of mustard around his mouth to one of the two teachers, long-haired girls in furry coats like her own. They seem to have lassoed her. Then she realizes it's a rope; they're clinging to a rope, with a teacher at each end, and she has got in the middle. What a good idea; little children will hold on if you tell them to.

The teachers untangle her and say, "Come along now," jerking the children briskly down the sidewalk. A small spectacled girl has a pink balloon floating from the end of her little finger. There are a lot of pairs of spectacles for such a small group of kindergarten-aged children.

The children are blind. These are blind children, with their teachers, sightless among the seeing, though she can't see any too well herself, in her dark glasses with the sun gone down, hurrying toward an uptown appointment.

The hot light. An egg, a shiny egg dancing in a glass. (Sunday morning she will burn the bacon and spill the scrambled eggs on the floor trying to stamp out the fire in her bedroom slippers.) Lying on a table, somebody cried, "Hey that hurts, it hurts," and yet it didn't hurt that much.

"Relax. Don't fight it," said the nurse. "Would you care for a cigarette? I'm afraid all I've got is Salems"—putting it between dry lips.

An involvement of the inner space, a truly savage pain. Slurp, water whizzing in the basin. Will it travel down the sewers like an abandoned pet, eyeless, lost to the gene pool, never to breed?

Doctor having left the room, his assistant matter-of-factly sprinkled water over what was in the basin, saying, "I baptize thee in the name of the Father and of the Son and of the Holy Ghost."

"You are baptizing a newt," she said reproachfully.

The nurse looked ashamed. "Sorry, but I just have to do this. Say, you know, I keep newts?"

"I have tropical fish, myself."

Let's go to bed and tell lies—almost there now. *Committing our murders decently, in private.* Punching the moon-white elevator button. The elevator boxes her into a private space; she rises with it, shaking in silence. I *don't know that he's you. You haven't heard he is me.*

He greets her at the door, waving a martini glass, reeling her into the party. "Oh my God, am I glad to see you," she says.

Wood

"I WANT TO FALL FROM THE HIGHEST BRANCH," said a young academic, spreading his arms to show how he would float through the June-green boughs, like a diver in leaf water. Though the jumping-off place was a good sixty feet from his head, pillowed comfortably on Arboretum grass, his friends, unpacking and handing around picnic food, couldn't help looking up. "A touch of anomie, Jay, buddy? It will pass," said Dave.

"We have met the anomie and he is ours," Jay murmured.

"He needs ballast," their old friend Arthur explained. "Have a meatball. Why don't you pass him a meatball, Laura?"

Now, Arthur's wife wasn't near the meatballs, though she hadn't missed any of the conversation. *I'm not about to ask him what he wants to fall for.* She was kneeling before a plastic basin full of soapy water trying to interest her daughter and the tree-diver's son in making bubbles, while they continued to throw bits of grass at each other; shortly one of the children would wail—hers.

"Don't reach for any high branches," her father used to say, but he wasn't from this country and his meaning was sometimes lost in translation.

The little girl had grass in her eye, and scrubbed at it, screaming, with a soapy hand. Her playmate looked frightened and ran to his father (his mother had rather suddenly left home, in order, she said, to find herself). Jay reached up and popped an olive into his son's mouth. Laura gently licked away the grass blade—an Old World remedy. "Let's see if we can't make the biggest soap bubble ever," she exclaimed, unhopefully; she had yet to taste any of the feast. She held the wire loop to the wind. An iridescent skin trembled, billowed, took on the size and shape of the moon in the sky, set itself free and sailed imperially over the picnic into a barberry bush. There was a bleat, which no one else heard, from her other baby, stashed like Moses in some tall grass near the oak tree.

The tree had a sign tacked to its bark: QUERCUS BICOLOR, *Origin Unknown (Spontaneous)*. Beneath it the picnickers were handing around paper plates full of chicken pieces, pickled peppers, stuffed tomatoes, home-made whole-wheat bread, white and yellow cheeses, plastic glasses of Lacrima d'Arno wine, and a joint. The acrophile, father of the grass-thrower, had renounced tobacco the same month when his wife renounced him. Jay took a mournful puff. "I want to be high, high, high. Don't anybody offer me a real weed. Don't you dare. Please?"

Dave's wife, Myra, found space for a tray of cold lasagna on the crowded tablecloth spread on the grass and unstable as a mattress. She had a baby on her back in a green canvas sling. Arthur's hand reached for the last of the meatballs, a garlic-studded lump that might have helped stabilize a zeppelin.

Laura returned, thrust a chicken leg into her daughter's hand, and, rescuing the Tears of the Arno from offering itself onto the grass, poured herself some. A gold bird whistled from the top of the tree. "Hark," said Jay.

"There it is." Arthur pointed upward with his fork. "See it, Laura?"

"An oriole, I believe," said Dave, always well informed.

"They've almost vanished, you know, because of DDT and fallout," said Myra, who knew even more than he did. The bird, whatever its origin, whistled a few more bars of its theme and flew on north, out of the Arboretum. Anchored in another, distant grove of trees, a red and a green kite nearly crossed the sun. Nearer the road, a Frisbee cut across the sky. Humming insects of many sorts were at work on every flowering tree.

Laura brushed one away from an endangered child. While edible things disappeared from the tablecloth, plastic and cellulose were multiplying there at a great rate. Mouths were busy. "The inequity of the present-day tenure system . . ." Dave was saying.

"The hyperborean angst of it," added Jay.

Myra recited to Arthur her meatball formula. Then she and Dave complained about their landlord, and Arthur about his, but not Jay, whose apartment had already been re-rented. The conversation switched to travel, and the fare to dessert, Myra's locally famous hand-cranked ice cream, accompanied by animal crackers, Laura's contribution. This was their last picnic before Jay took a plane to Europe: Holland, he thought. Jay's college had given him the summer off, maybe even permanently off. "It's not one of your bigger countries," he noted, holding his hands six inches apart. "But there are those that love it."

"Particularly tulip farmers."

"And uncles."

"The food is a bit on the heavy side," Myra said.

"They're strong on weaving and home crafts," it was agreed. "And elm disease," said Dave.

"They love to skate; in winter it's the only way to get around," said Laura's husband. "Be sure to bring your skates, Jay."

Laura saw her other baby come crawling toward her.

Jay was going to spend the summer with a family and learn Dutch; perhaps, come winter, he would teach there. The Netherlandish tongue should be a snap to learn, since it was really only bad German. "Of course, I don't know German."

German, Arthur pointed out, was simply bad English.

Jay said, with a sigh, he would miss the kid (who would be living with his grandparents). He looked at Laura, her dark head bent over a child in her lap and one in her arms, refusing his milk bottle. Myra began to put the covers back on the covered dishes. Arthur and Jay finished the last of the ice cream. Arthur told Myra she should open a restaurant. "We've thought about it, old friend," Dave said. They were serious; it would be a place where not just you and your friends but your friends' parents and their friends would all want to dine. Arthur's father-in-law was in the restaurant business; the friends could be partners. Laura said nothing, which made it three-to-one in favor. *Haven't we got enough to do already?*

Myra, who made everything from scratch, even chocolate candy, woke her baby and began to nurse it.

"Is there any more wine?"

"Or pot?"

A Great Dane with a Frisbee in its mouth loped through the trees, scaring the babies. Dave and Myra were going to tour the French wine country that summer. Dave's tenure might not have been confirmed, but what of that?

"Great. We'll meet you there for a picnic in August. And Jay can skate over from the Lowlands. Doesn't that sound like a good vacation, Laura?" She smiled. *With these kids? We're not going anywhere.*

Blond Arthur said, "That one will never live to grow up," after being shot in the seat of the pants by a professor's child with a gun that fired suction-cupped darts, while he and Jay were eating sandwiches by the river after classes, their last spring as undergraduates. He ran after the monster and right into Laura, flying a strangely shaped kite with the help of the river wind and her friend Anne. Laura had wind-flushed cheeks, a haughty nose, and a figure she pretended not to know about. Immediately he offered her half a sandwich.

When she first went to the northern college she was cold all the time, and wore dark glasses as though the sun were still shining, and coils and coils of knitted muffler up to the glasses. Her immigrant father had taken her south after his wife died, where there was a married cousin, and liked it so much better than New York he never returned, but went to work as a waiter in a fish restaurant and presently owned it, and then several. Her Aunt Livia, who had heard about the winters, knitted a woolen scarf; her father, more skillful with his hands than with words, had taught her to build a kite.

There was nothing left to eat; they got up from the picnic and carted the rubbish to the wire basket by the road, overflowing with the remains of other repasts. Jay and Arthur and Dave encircled, and attempted to climb, a maple *(ACER PSEUDO-PLATANUS)*, while the older children chased round it like squirrels, but the lowest branches were out of reach.

They wandered to the top of a hill and clambered down the other side. "Carry me, carry me," sang the children. The light was turning rose.

"What do you want to be?" unquiet Anne had asked her once when they were still green, walking to the river together in the sound of bells.

No one had ever suggested to Laura that she wasn't something. So she'd never thought about it.

When Arthur said, "Marry me, come home with me," she said, "I don't know, I have to ask my father": he had a heart attack. By the time she was graduated she still didn't know. Both Jay and Arthur wanted to marry her, Jay with his pining heart, Arthur who got what he wanted.

Being out of school was nearly as tedious as being in it. While she considered, *Shall I go to graduate school? Shall I go back home?* Arthur got his draft notice. When her father learned they were engaged he had another heart attack. She flew south; he offered her money to travel. Laura traveled through a number of countries and met more of her relatives. Arthur's letters followed her from American Express to American Express, along with her father's checks from home. (Arthur stayed out of the Army because he had a rare blood type.) When she got sick from traveling so much Arthur caught up with her and brought her back, and she became his wife. What else was there for her to become? Jay married Anne.

Dragging her children downhill, she followed the others to the weeping beech, the only tree of its kind in the Arboretum. Heart-shaped leaves on slender outer branches brushed the grass; within their shade, around the immense roots, the ground was bare and dark. Jay had already lifted his son and himself past the gray-white trunk where scores of other climbers had carved initials and signs. Myra was up there. Dave, and Arthur. They helped her up onto a lower bough wide as a bench, from which, through the leaves, was visible a twist of the little stream that watered the Arboretum. Left behind, children murmured at the base.

The others were out of sight, hidden in the green cave. Laura leaned against springy, sustaining branches. "I could sit here all night," she said.

"Careful," came Jay's voice. "This is a sacred tree." Was he going to threaten to fall out of it? "The beech is sacred to Apollo."

Her daughter was jumping up and down looking for her; Laura hauled her up, and passed her to Arthur, several crotches higher. Cross-legged on the weeping beech, she was smiled upon by her husband. "No, you meatball," he said to Jay, "the beech is sacred to Zeus."

"What do you want to be when you grow up, Arthur?"

Little Laurie squirmed down to her mother and clung to her with twig-thin, slippery arms; the baby came to and, kneeling, tried to worm his upper part around the tree toward them, like a jealous inchworm.

"Satisfied, by Jove," said Arthur. "What do you want to be . . . Myra?"

"Me? Oh, competent." The tree rustled, as if to ratify her wish.

"David?"

"Tenured."

Laura touched the many-times-desecrated bark. A child's thin arms are as tough as vines. They came with marriage; spontaneous, unknown. *Not to be married! Not to* be *anything!*

"Jay?"

"In love," he whispered. "With someone like Anne. I want the whole painful relationship all over again."

* * * * *

"Laura? Laura, where are you?" Arthur called, the traces of an Armenian sandwich about the corners of his mouth. They were on their way out of the Arboretum. The stream had frozen into a watery-margined S with many cracks and bubbles; oak and beech leaves, preserved over winter by their tannin, floated under the ice surface. Footprints led in all directions across the snowy field, but besides him and his children no other souls were to be seen.

"Arthur, can't you ever wipe your mouth?" Laura appeared from a birch grove where she'd been fruitlessly searching for kindling wood. "The one thing I can't stand about Arthur is, he never wipes his mouth," she told her children.

Arthur never stayed hurt for long. "We forgot the baklava. Laura, you left it in the glove compartment."

"No, Arthur, we *ate* the baklava."

"Well, there were a couple of pieces left." He had an empty canvas sack slung over one shoulder and peered behind to see if the children were keeping up; they were, Laurie sucking her thumb and the little boy doing okay for a toddler—soon he'd want to be carried. February sunlight, unconstrained by the gates of leaves, flickered off Arthur's hair, going a little at the top.

They came to a thicket of water-loving trees, slender willows named *Salix discolor, lucida, babylonica, gracilis.* The little girl put her foot through the ice and cried because she'd broken it. The willow branches were almost forsythia-yellow, and covered with furry catkins. Laura pushed her sunglasses up over her forehead. "You know, my father never believed you when you said that plant was named 'pussy willow.'"

Arthur kept his eyes peeled for fallen branches, but the caretakers of the Arboretum, an invisible but hard-working force, had apparently spirited away every twig. "I'm hungry," he said.

"He's always hungry." She wasn't, any more.

Though it was too early for their flowering, the maples were red with shiny buds. Following the rivulet, the long way around, would lead to the gate, but Arthur knew a shortcut. So they ducked through bushes *(Rhus aromatica, Hydrangea arborescens)*, on a gradually ascending slope, and Arthur, carrying his son, read out their names as if they were directions, and carefully restrained the longer branches from swinging back and scratching their faces. Around them now were leafless lindens and maples; Arthur pointed to an *Acer saccharum* from which a little juice had begun to leak and noted, "The sap is rising." Over toward the top of the hill, on a ledge of its own, a tree so weirdly twisted in limb and twig it seemed to be trying to turn itself out was scribbled upon the light sky and snow. Something dark was impaled within its branches halfway up, an old kite or a squirrel's nest.

"Where did that tree come from?" asked Arthur. He could not locate its name anywhere on the thorny trunk. "Dave, where are you now that we need you?" (In St. Louis, where he and Myra had gone to open an organic restaurant, his college, after granting him his professorship, having abruptly folded.) He laughed. "Well, I guess it's someone's idea of a tree who never saw one."

"It's a womandrake," Laura said, not laughing. She pulled her sunglasses back over her eyes. Her father had returned, that winter, to the old country, where, he said, he wished to be buried.

The little girl couldn't take her eyes off it. "Maybe she thinks it's a witch, too," Arthur said. "I think it's just cold. In the summer it will straighten out and be just like the other trees."

Laurie shivered. "Let's go *home*."

"You see, Arthur, she *can* talk."

The little girl ran ahead; Arthur put his son down and he scurried with commendable steadiness after his sister. They passed a Japanese magnolia, gray with hairy cocoons nearly ready to split. Arthur stopped and pretended to read the label. He had been prepared to like his father-in-law, once they got acquainted, but whenever the old man came to visit, spoiling the grandchildren, talking his own language to Laura, she became stiff, detached, a perfect stranger.

His stomach rumbled; he looked around with shame—they were walking ahead. He caught up. Both children had crash-landed and were being quieted. He went down in the snow and made an angel. He bounced up with snow in his hair. "Look! Rabbit tracks—" which could have been those of anything, from a squirrel to a lion. Wherever anything had stepped, the snow was so frail that spikes of green appeared. "There was someone who always hated the sight of grass in the snow," Laura said.

"Your father?" Though the old man had invariably stayed away in wintertime.

She squinted. "Anne—" Her restless friend whose postcard tracks were fading month by month.

Their daughter discovered a neat pile of willow and maple discards raked together and somehow overlooked by the caretakers. Arthur rummaged through it for branches that seemed long and alive. "If we put these in water, I'll bet they root, and we can plant them outside." He started to gather them into the empty sack.

"What is he doing with those things?" Laura asked. "Leave them alone. They'll never grow."

Whenever he reached out toward her now she turned away. *Oh, my wife. I want a wife.*

They were midway down the slope that stretched obtusely toward the wall beyond which the car was parked; hundreds of purplish footprints upon it and otherwise vacant. Carrying on his back his slim gleanings, Arthur licked a finger and touched the wind. "This would be a good place to fly kites."

"Whatever made you think of that?"

"Don't you remember that picnic, when we flew the kites?"

"We weren't flying any kites. I was blowing soap bubbles."

One windy Easter while they were still students, younger, good friends, unmarried, Laura showed them all how to make kites from sticks and colored tissue paper. They rode out with food on motorcycles to a muddy plowed meadow in the country and flew them. The trees were filmy with new leaves and the earth smelled almost overpoweringly of growth. One, two, three, four, five, six kites sprang up, rattling tissue-paper tails, transparent and colored like church windows—rose, violet, topaz, chartreuse, orange, sky. Dave told Myra she needed more tail and they argued about aeronautics while Arthur's kite broke out of bounds, crossed lines with Anne's; both fell like damaged butterflies into the trees at the edge of the farmer's field. Jay's caught in a low-hanging locust branch. Laura's soared as high as the string would let it; they attached the remnants of Jay's on it and it went up some more; they added tail, scientifically, more string, and took turns flying it until their hands were blistered. Around a quarter to five the wind died down and they reeled it in. How they could run in those days!

Where Anne found herself these days was hard to make out from the blurred postmarks. Jay was too rapturously unhappy, he wrote, with a lonely American exile in Düsseldorf even to think about repatriation.

"Let's come back here the first warm day," Arthur suggested.

She shook her head. "They'd get caught in the leaves. Anyway I've forgotten how to make them." So, of course, she hadn't.

Arthur took a child's hand in each of his, and rolled them down the slope in a flurry of arms, till gravity arrested them and they picked themselves up.

There was a restless, trustless woman who had packed her suitcase with clothes for a week's vacation and never returned to her family. How was that possible?

Laura stood unmoving, the trees at her back, and the little girl wanted to start uphill in her direction but Arthur insisted, "Let's hurry or they'll lock us in. She'll catch up. Oh, look what Nero's found." The baby was bent over a large heart drawn into the snow, left over from Valentine's Day. God alone knew how many were inscribed, indelibly, on the bark of the Arboretum.

His wife was still far away. Arthur put his fingers in his pockets to warm them and discovered a sticky piece of baklava, which he ate with great satisfaction.

Visitors

ACROSS FROM WHERE THE OLD JAIL USED TO STAND, the Women's House of Detention, there still is a pastry shop, with windows along the sidewalk so you can eat your croissants or sundae with chicory-flavored French coffee and watch the passers-by, and they can look in at you. A small woman with olive skin and sleek black hair is sitting on one of the heart-backed chairs, sharing a brioche with a little girl who will grow up to look just like her, whose beauty is yet trapped behind wires on her teeth and spectacles too large for her face and smidgeon of a nose. They display exaggerated pleasure with each other's company. The little girl has her head thrown back in laughter, and the mother's elbows, in a green-and-red Paisley print blouse with the cuffs rolled up, are planted on the little table; her shoulders shake with laughter. Her red spring coat is draped over the back of the chair. Even in this polyglot quarter of town they appear exotic, Continental. A hand raps on the glass to attract the attention of somebody inside: she looks up, in exaggerated surprise, and it is clearly not Henrietta Gordon at all.

* * * * *

Once upon a time—stories often begin—Henrietta was reading a letter from an acquaintance, aloud, in her living room in an old apartment house not far from that shop. She was standing very straight, and she wore a dressing gown of dark-red velvety material that reached exactly to the floor, so she seemed to have no feet, like a museum doll on a pedestal. There was a knock at the door.

"Oh, it's you," she said, as if she were expecting someone else. Her eyes glittered like black mirrors. "You can join us for tea. Bob's taken the kids uptown and Esther and I are waiting for them to come back. I'd take your coat, but the doctor said not to lift. Listen—"

The sun had gone to the other side of the building and the living room was dim, but Henrietta hardly needed light to read by; she had apparently got the letter by heart. Her two guests drank hot smoky tea as they listened.

"When I asked him if he found it tedious, he said, 'I am not bored, Anna. The nurses read to me; I have a radio. But mostly I like to imagine things. Most of the time I'm not really here at all. There's a window next to my bed. Below my window there's a field, and beyond that more fields, and then hills, valleys and towns, and over the last hill, the sea; and in the fields there are white horses pasturing, racing the clouds. I lean out and whistle to them and they come galloping up to my window, on their backs a troupe of little people; they invite me to ride away with them, all of us on white horses. My horse drinks from the stream. I swim him across a river. I follow the little people all day, riding across the prairies, till at night we come to a gated town, our horses are fed, and we are welcomed in. We sit up half the night telling stories of where we've been; we carry the news from town to town. . . . Every morning when I wake, I wonder, Where will they take me today?'

"The drugs stimulated him to some extent but I believe also it was a way of accepting the letting go, riding farther and farther each day, till he wasn't afraid of the distance any more. And then one day he just didn't bother to return."

It was a first-rate performance; almost she had them believing it was her own parent, her own words. She returned the letter proudly to its envelope, and let her arms drop, like folded wings. "Can't you hear them—the horses? Coming closer?"

But the only sound was of a car backing out of a parking space on the street eight stories down.

"They're mine!"

"*No*, Henrietta," said Esther, reasonably. "Do sit down and have some of this nice tea. English Breakfast, isn't it?"

"Earl Grey. How can I sit down with this bad back?"

"Your back's much better. Why, last week you couldn't get out of bed."

"The chiropractor in New Jersey ruined my back," Henrietta explained, in case there was any one of her acquaintances who wasn't familiar with the story, or had forgotten it. In manipulating her spine he had caused it to go in where it was supposed to go out. Feel. . . . You see! So she had gone to another man who gave her an injection of Novocain and had her do an exercise. "Since then I can't feel my back at all. I can't feel anything. My tooth that's supposed to hurt doesn't hurt!" Carefully she lowered herself to the Oriental carpet, and stretched out in its exact center—she might almost have been part of the design. And not just quacks, real doctors, respected members of the medical profession had betrayed her, too. One had attacked her; another, whom she'd believed in, promised he wouldn't put her under when she went to him with an ear abscess, and he did. "I trusted him like a father!"

Well, her friends said, doctors—recalling experiences of their own with doctors, both colorful and grotesque.

"You see!" said Henrietta.

Which didn't mean she shouldn't trust the ones who said she'd get well. Who *insisted* she get well while Henrietta resisted with every ounce of strength—her husband, her child, her friends and comforters, her doctors. The pills which made her ankles swell, the whirlpool treatments in the Out-Patients' Clinic, the hypnotist, the acupuncture needles that gave her a rash, the psychiatrist. The off-color dreams, the transference, the yellow capsules that lifted her spirits so she ran after a Madison Avenue bus and tumbled down, jarring vertebrae in her lower spine.

Animated, even gay now, she brought out on a Sèvres dish a batch of wheat-germ cookies she had taught her daughter, Kitten, to make that morning, in the well-furnished kitchen, cluttered with unemptied grocery boxes. From it, when—no, if—she could bend and lift again, would come streaming stollen and pfeffernuesse, springerles, and ginger-bread to decorate and give to friends and to hang on the nondenom-inational holiday tree that would stand beside the blue-tiled fireplace. (Henrietta's friends had all urged her to do a cookbook; she even had a contract with a publisher, and it was half completed, illustrations and all. But she had put it aside to write poetry in a workshop at the Y.) She sighed. "It's impossible, this numbness, like when I was taking those mood-elevators. I couldn't feel, I couldn't know where I was going." She perched on the Moroccan hassock and ate a cookie.

Somewhere in the building the machinery of the ancient lift began to creak; Esther gathered her long skirt around her ankles—maybe it was Bob returning with the two children. Over by the window which over-looked a courtyard and bare ailanthus tree some light came through onto an easel with the unfinished canvas of a child against a heavily stippled background. "We started that last summer," Henrietta said. "I thought: the black is for her black-hearted mummy, the green for her youth. Goodness, I forgot to feed Kitten's snake. Want to see?"

Down the hall, and beneath a bulletin board tacked up with an expert child's drawings, was a terrarium containing sand, a log, and a very thin snake staring down what was otherwise a cheerful room. Extracting a bug from a flour canister with a pair of tweezers, Henrietta said, "It just doesn't seem to eat. Poor Kitten, if it dies." The snake looked the other way. "They'll have to operate, I'm sure of it."

"On the snake?"

"On me." A deep line appeared between her eyebrows. "I'm probably allergic to anesthetic."

"You are not. You must make up your mind to get well. For Kitten's sake."

"And Bob's, I know. They hardly see me anymore. I'm always in there—" flinging out an arm toward the open door to the other room, the folded laundry piled on Biedermeier chairs, canvases stacked face to the wall, the secretary where Henrietta used to write love poems and copy recipes, and the bed that never got made, a book spread, binding upward, on the pillow. What was she reading—*The Primal Scream*? Sylvia Plath? The *I Ching*? An old-fashioned picture book: *Struwwel-peter*.

"My God, that used to give me nightmares," Ethel said. "Is it Kitten's?"

"She brought it from the library and I confiscated it, of course. My mother used to read it to me in German. Let's read it aloud!" So they took the book into the living room and, sitting close together on the long, upholstered couch, the better to see by the single light from the standing lamp, passed the book around, laughing and shuddering over the story of the Scissors Man and the Boy Who Sucked His Thumb, and Henrietta read best and laughed the most. "No more," cried Esther. "It's sick. Henrietta. You *are* going to go to Connecticut tomorrow?"

"Maybe not for the entire weekend."

"It would be so good for you to get away from this. A change. For all of you."

"We'll see." Henrietta held up to the lamp one of her small, firm hands. "Do you believe in palmistry? A gypsy told me my lifeline was crossed, that something would happen to me in the middle of my life to immobilize me forever. Let me see your hands," taking theirs with cold fingers.

Then a key turned in the door, the police lock slid back in its bolt, and Bob came in with Kitten and Esther's Wendy. By this time it was quite dark outside the window; he moved around the living room, switching on lamps, erasing the long shadows. Light warmed the room, yellowed their faces, the children going to their mothers, telling about their afternoon, skating at Rockefeller Center—Kitten more solemn of the two, light glinting off her spectacles. "Mummy, Bob said on the bus when I sneezed that I must have a guitar. Actually he said *catarrh*, but Wendy and I didn't understand. It was so *funny.*" Henrietta hugged her for a moment.

"Bob, was she sneezing? Did you see that she kept her coat buttoned?"

The visitors got up to leave. Bob helped them on with their coats. "How nice to see you again." He pressed his cheek against theirs. "Come around again soon. It does her a world of good." Esther went back to fetch Wendy. "We're going to the country tomorrow, you know. Things could be worse." He gave a little laugh.

"Bob," called Henrietta from the bathroom, "I can't find the thermometer. I'm sure this child is coming down with something."

* * * * *

Henrietta's paintings could have been good. They were going to be, anyway. They were much better than anything she wrote, the scraps of poems that filled the secretary pigeonholes, the letters she sent out, all over the country, to California and Oregon and Mexico and even Germany, on airmail paper with italic script so black it went through to the other side. Much better than the notes she didn't mail.

Bob called up all her friends: "I have to tell you that Henrietta—" He sounded as though he had been running.

"I can't believe it." But, after a moment, they all could.

"Kitten was a wreck. . . ."

"Did she get over her cold?"

"She didn't have a cold. I was a wreck. She thought it would be so good for us to go to the country. She was going to bring her sketch pad— she was all *packed.* Saturday morning, Saturday morning the car was at the door, and she said, 'My back will never take the trip. *You* go. You need a break more than I do.' So we went. We called her Saturday night and she sounded fine, she sounded cheerful. When we came back yesterday afternoon, and the chain on the door was off the hook, so that we could get inside, I knew."

The first note said: "Don't go any further until you read this."

"I told Kitten to go down to the lobby and pick up the mail. She was lying cold as a fish on the floor beside the bed. Our friend the doctor couldn't revive her. Then the police came."

There was one for Bob, one for her mother, one for her ex-analyst, one for Kitten.

* * * * *

At this same time of year, but several years earlier, a young family and two friends from New York who were suffering from jet lag were sunning themselves beside a swimming pool in California. The husbands had been classmates, and they'd attended each other's weddings.

"How can you bear not to live *here?*" asked Vicky, the hostess, wiggling her toes at the benign sun. Her children, one of them named after the college roommate, were splashing in the shallow end of the pool, fearless as penguins; the five-year-old was teaching her baby brother to swim under water.

"Hey-hey, I think she's trying to drown him," said Skip, getting up to refill their glasses. Not gilded like Vicky and the kids, wearing a huge straw hat to protect his balding pate, he twirled the tray expertly on the palm of his hand like a waiter, which he had once been in college, did a quick two-step, shoved up the back of his hat with the free hand, and shuffled off to the kitchen.

A palm tree bent in applause. Vicky went to restore order in the pool. "Why *don't* we live here?" asked the wife who was visiting, stifling a yawn. "I'll bet those children have never had a cold in their lives."

"They have each had one," Vicky said, returning and settling back in a pool chair. "I hated New York the year I was at Barnard, my face was always dirty. Still, there was much going *on*. Nothing ever goes on here except movie openings." The faintest disturbance of her impeccable American Girl brow—was it possible to be bored in Paradise?

The New York wife was enviously taking in the surroundings. "Look what you have that we haven't. A pool, a garden, a sky, a chance for children to *run.*"

"Smog," Vicky said, devil's advocate.

"Trade it for Air Unsatisfactory. Palms, outdoor barbecues, year-round tans, good schools, vitamin C—"

"The La Brea Tar Pits," added the husband.

"Whereas we have landlords, garbage strikes—"

"Museums," said Vicky, who had been an art major. "The New York Ballet, good restaurants, X-rated movies, a chance to—"

"Get mugged?"

"I guess you're right. Nothing bad ever happens here."

"Except leukemia," said Skip, dumping the tray of drinks on a wicker table.

Yes, his friends, he was an X-rated body, and nobody east of the Mississippi was to know. Sing no sad songs for Skip!

Lit like a demon over the steaks that he was barbecuing for the four of them after the children were sleeping; the lights of Los Angeles around the dark sky; hot fat sputtering on the charcoal briquets. "Oh, perfection," Vicky sighed. They drank a good deal of vintage Margaux, Skip holding the bottles unprofessionally over the flames so they could inspect the label. "I'm suffocating," he said suddenly and jumped into the pool. His hat floated to the surface like a lily pad.

* * * * *

The friends of Henrietta sat at high noon in a cool dark room carpeted in blue, on folding chairs, among plastic flowers, studying each other and waiting for a sign. A dog barked and barked over the traffic sounds outside. The receptionist in an adjoining room quoted burial prices over the telephone.

"Could you pass me the Rolaids?" someone whispered.

"That's her mother." An amber-haired lady with a lacquered coiffure entered, was helped to a seat in the front row, her face guarded like a critic's.

"Is the child going to come?"

"God, I hope not."

One of the undertakers, a tall young man with neat little caterpillars of sideburns, escorted a visitor into the Viewing Room, both of them whispering.

"That's Vince Nicksen, their Best Man. He's going to read the poems if Bob can't."

Having given him a peep at the setup, the undertaker withdrew to his office to discuss terms with the viewer, a prospective client. The dog barked, chairs creaked, the telephone rang, and outside in the sunlight construction workers began to tear up a patch of sidewalk. "We start at three hundred and forty dollars, and you may come in and personally inspect our line of—"

Vince Nicksen arrived.

Concealed fluorescent lights illuminated the real roses on top of the coffin, which occupied a platform or stage at the front of the room, framed on either side by black curtains. To its right, between Henrietta's bier and the people on the chairs, stood the lectern from which her young husband finally spoke in a drenched but confident voice, reading Henrietta's verses, publishing for the first and only time her words.

* * * * *

"My dearest little Kitten," his child read. "Oh please believe how very much I love you, even if it doesn't seem so. You must never think this had anything to do with not loving me enough. You are lovely and lively and kind.

Even your mistakes are shining ones. It breaks my heart to think that I can't stay to see you grow up, but I would only spoil it for you. It is this illness. . . ." She put it in her top dresser drawer and fed her snake, and was playing catch with Wendy now in their schoolyard, dazzled by the low, hard rays of the sun and trying to keep her glasses from sliding down the bridge of her nose.

* * * * *

Wait. Through the Park a young woman came pedaling as fast as she could, late again; the games started at 5:30. She had a bunch of school papers to correct in her satchel and some in her bicycle basket which began to whip away from it into the drifted leaves, but she lowered her head and drove on, unimpeded by pedestrians on the Mall, her shadow streaming behind her under the street lamps. At the verge of the ball field she flung her bike down and began to run, tripping over the frozen, pitted ground, sobbing for breath. "I'm here, I'm here—" she had reached the center of the field, the diamond gouged into the grass, home plate. "I'm ready to play." But she was too late, or early: the players had retired for the season. And instead of cheers she heard the mutinous howl of a siren, and the earth was heaving. Soon her name would be in the papers.

During the summer, when a group of office workers used to play slow-pitch Softball after hours, Melaine, cycling home through the Park, rode up and tossed her bike on the grass and exchanged amiable words with the team captain, and her father, but could never be persuaded to join the game. She might take a swig of beer as the scores mounted on both sides, keeping one hand protectively on the brown satchel that looked almost too big for her to carry. Then she would strap it on the fender of the bicycle and ride away under a skyful of gulls out of the park, downtown to her apartment.

Melanie Moore, 23.

The players ran round the bases, another run batted in! The sky would be cluttering up with the horsehead shapes of clouds, someone flying a kite among them, the grass in the Sheep Meadow wasted with heat and the pressure of gym shoes, tiny players, far off, at other games. With enormous, lustrous eyes Melanie appreciatively watched the grownups' sport, and every Tuesday her shadow was longer and thinner. She never stayed till the end. They had an undefeated season.

If they had to write to her parents, what should they say? Well, that she always had her eye on the ball, she seemed to be having a good time, she looked beautiful and loved.

She was loved, all right. She lived in the same apartment house as her parents, in a tidy rent-controlled studio furnished with things they'd given her, eagerly, anxiously trying out different men and classes. She couldn't teach them enough, that was what worried her. Then love went West, in the form of Henry. At Sunday dinners with her parents and brothers and sisters, they saw she was suffering from a greensickness, and filled her plate with extra helpings. Her friends and associates knew better.

"It's a bad trip, Melly."

"A bummer."

"No way."

The papers were full of statistics: war casualties, murders, accidents. (Fatalities from every cause appeared to be on the increase.) All over the city more young people were administering to themselves drugs obtained with no doctor's prescription; not always because they were poor.

For example, a doctor informed the press, a girl in her early twenties, from an affluent family, had been experimenting with the intravenous use of certain painkillers for several months. Boils developed at the site of injection, the inside of her arm. Golden-colored staphylococci rode through her bloodstream and began to eat at her heart. Blood clots from the damaged heart valve broke away and migrated to the lungs, rupturing air sacs and forming abscesses that resulted in high fever and labored breathing. "Despite treatment with tens of millions of units of morphine—"

"Mother," cried the girl in the ambulance, "don't let them give me morphine!" Which was their first clue.

It would have been a lie to write that she'd been happy.

* * * * *

Skip's remission continued until even the doctors began to hope, though none of them ever used the word "cure." With the money Vicky's father gave them and Skip's own good salary, they proceeded to live it up, weekends at Tahoe, skiing at Vail, picnics at the race track—Skip was a gambler, and so lucky he had to pay taxes on his winnings. They bought a race horse and a share in a French vineyard, and Vicky tried not to cling to him too intensely at night, but sometimes they overdid it anyway and he stayed home the following day. High-hearted Vicky, whom he'd plucked from Barnard soft with love when she was only nineteen and he an old man of twenty-three, had cooperated with all his schemes from the time of her first, memorable meeting with his parents, decked out with false wax teeth and a fright wig: "Mom, Dad, I'd like you to meet my fiancée." Vo-dee-o-do.

He couldn't help it, he *had* to turn to someone he knew slightly in a crowded elevator saying, "Isn't it a shame about Roosevelt Grier? I hear he ruptured his liver," just as the doors opened at his floor. Always eager to please, he arranged a blind date for a timid colleague with a stunning young woman, who first showed up in the colleague's office as a divorce client with a marital history that laid his ears back; that evening, in the restaurant, as arranged by the go-between: "Why, I believe we've met before!"

The joker came up, the wild card, no bluffing, called his hand. He wanted to stay out of the hospital until after Thanksgiving. Thanksgiving night a blood vessel burst in his knee; hot packs and cold compresses couldn't touch the pain and finally he yielded.

"Hey-hey-hey, don't feel so good," he said in a muffled voice over Long Distance. He insisted that everything be done to make the odds more favorable. Much of the time he was delirious. Vicky lived in the hospital for six weeks. Once he turned to her and said in his normal voice, "I can't stand it." She held on to his hand as he begged her never to be unfaithful. He minded leaving her the worst, though her eyes were caves and her tanned skin pitted and caught to her healthy bones and she weighed a hundred and four pounds. On the last day of his life he ate a big meal.

His friends from the east, on their way to Los Angeles, were in midair, eating food off airline trays, when he died. At Vicky's house, full of food and company, they all toasted Skip. "Wasn't he funny?"

"He died laughing."

* * * * *

It was over. Almost. Henrietta's husband made sure everybody had a car to ride in. The cars stood by, double-parked, motors idling while the driver changed a flat tire on the hearse; then they drove with headlights on to a town no one had ever heard of, way across the Hudson, for an hour and a half, Henrietta, in her rented carriage, at the head of the procession.

"Once she was going to go out to our place on the Island, alone, to paint and think," Esther said. "We rented a car so I could drive her, because of course she couldn't take the train."

Because she couldn't bend her back. The Best Man, a doctor, had found her with her knees drawn up, in her red robe on the floor, like a sleeping child.

"We were on the Belt Parkway when she said, 'Stop! I'm not ready to go after all.' So we turned back. I wonder if she was meaning to do it that weekend. The notes weren't dated. She could have written them any time." Pro-forma letters of resignation handed in to the administrator in case they should be needed.

"There was no way to reason with her," somebody said. "She was all peaks and troughs."

"She was a true romantic."

"She was afraid to grow old."

They passed through the iron gates of a cemetery somewhere in Bergen County, left the cars and assembled in the road edged with wintry bushes: where the green stopped and the mud began. Earthworks and ditches were all about the landscape. Bob was leading them across a wide brown field to the far side, where they could see a wall, and hear cars speeding by. The company picked its way over gravel, mud, and a bridge of boards to the open trench, braced with pipes and wide enough for six coffins, and there was Henrietta's, pumped up on a jack. In the distance a yellow bulldozer was filling in a hole.

They strained to hear: the rabbi's brief eulogy, the well-used prayers, the whispers of friends. "That's Tim Rich; he flew in from San Diego"—a bare-headed man in a topcoat, reminded by Henrietta in one of her widely flung messages, of their grand past, before Bob, with all its peaks and troughs. Like all of them, he had wanted to save her.

And, again in the front row, the woman with the elegant hair, who had been incarcerated by the Nazis before the war, and, for a week, was permitted visitors; one afternoon she put on a visitor's coat and walked out when visiting hours ended. She was a survivor.

The contraption let the box down between the pipes and as the guests trod gingerly back to the cars the hungry bulldozer moved in. None of them had the remotest idea of the name of the place they'd left Henrietta.

* * * * *

But that's not all. For out in the suburbs, that winter, a woman with an exhausted face opened the door to a visitor who had come by with a pot of flowers, cellar-raised. "Aw. Now wasn't that thoughtful. Come in and help me find a place to put them." They waded through the wrapping paper and empty boxes piled in the entrance hall to the cavernous living room, papered in many shades of brown, where all the chairs had been pulled back to the walls and some had fallen over. From a stained-glass ceiling fixture emanated rays of colored crepe paper which could have been hung only by a man with an eight-foot reach atop a five-foot stepladder. Peter got up with effort from a brown leather reclining chair where he was nursing a coffee cup: "Let me take it, Maeve," receiving what were only some plants in a Woolworth's pot as if they were the last of their race, carrying them to a windowed recess with a built-in shelf where other plants in baskets and pots soaked up the outdoor light before it could penetrate far into the room. He put a child's teddy bear on the floor and the hyacinths where it had been. "There. You can smell them even if you can't see them. 'If you have two loaves of bread—' "

" 'Sell one and buy white hyacinths,' " said Mrs. Ryan, sinking into his chair and drinking his coffee. "I guess you can see we were having a birthday party. You missed it. That's either the good news or the bad news." The Ryans had, at last count, eleven children, so birthdays around there weren't even news.

Beyond her, in the dining room, under more crepe-paper streamers, the birthday boy was still at the table, sitting with his hands over his ears contemplating the remains of a cake, moving his head back and forth *no, no,* as if it were the wrong flavor. He was wearing a conical hat of shiny paper, fastened under the chin with a loop of rubber band. He was now sixteen years old.

Maeve Ryan got up to let Peter sit down again. "I was talking to this priest who addressed the Altar Guild last week," she said, conversationally. "The theme of his address was that God had a plan for pain, that it was a meaningful part of the scheme of things. So I asked him nicely if he could explain what exactly *was* the meaning of pain, and he said, 'God wills it,' and I asked, 'Why? What is the meaning of pain?' What is the meaning of pain?" she cried, thrusting her face up in challenge. "You tell me. What's it for?"

"Easy, Maeve."

The Ryans' next-to-youngest, Agnes, was upstairs in bed with a cold. Maeve had dosed her with aspirin just before the guests came. She slept right through the party; she slept through everything. Peter had put his hand on her forehead at three o'clock; her temperature was down. When the visitor left, Peter picked up the chairs and Maeve went upstairs to their bedroom, where she put the children when they were sick, with a cup of tea on a tray, but Aggie was no longer breathing.

The church was jammed, as it usually was after a minor atrocity, and, following the Mass of the Angels, people whispered, "If only it could have been Kevin."

The Ryans decided to sell, now most of the children were grown or gone, their white elephant of a house and move to California, to make a new start. They could get a better price, said the real-estate woman, if they fixed it up. Where to begin? Maeve papered, and Peter was layering new plaster onto the master bedroom ceiling when he touched his chest and went crashing off the ladder to the floor.

This time, they only said, "Luckily, she has her faith to support her."

And, now the house was really on the market, it was soon snapped up by a family with growing daughters who prized it for its high ceilings, many rooms, sturdy beams, and solid foundations. They planned to make Peter's plant nook into a whole wall of windows. Closing day they shook Maeve's hand in the real-estate agent's office, and that night two of their girls were returning in a taxi from a party through the mists of Mamaronek when a car driven by a doctor skidded and bumped into theirs and knocked them into the shrubbery. The taxi driver got off with a bloody nose, but the two girls flew out of the back seat like birds into a privet hedge, and the younger was in critical condition at County Hospital, Johanna their eldest D.O.A., the doctor with a broken arm—

* * * * *

Enough. Scientists in laboratories make things happen. They aim speedy, invisible particles at each other and call the marks of their disintegration "events." Atomic happenings pursue uniform and inevitable paths. Not human events. So what really happened is:

Bob and Kitten made an early return from Connecticut. Without being told, Kitten went to the kitchen phone and dialed 911, the emergency number, while Bob applied all the correct resuscitative measures. Henrietta's cookbook will be published this summer.

Skip, after five years, is still in remission—technically if not actually "cured"—and has mailed a Polaroid photograph of their daughter, stroking a horse's neck and wearing a red ribbon she has been awarded for show jumping, to their friends in New York, where the air has improved somewhat.

Agnes Mary Ryan's picture is in her high-school yearbook, and any day now Peter will do something about that ceiling. While the people in Mamaronek have two more children—their family is getting big as the Ryans'—and are searching for an even larger house.

* * * * *

But two blocks from where Henrietta lived, Melanie's mother is emptying Melanie's apartment, carrying whatever's of no use into the street to be retrieved by the garbage collectors if other scavengers don't collect it first. She's brushing dust off her clothes. "It's taken us a long time to get around to it. Well." Briskly, "The other stuff goes to the bin."

"Hey, Mom, look at this great glove I just found," says one of her boys, standing at the top of the steps and pounding a catcher's mitt with his right fist. It is May, and the ailanthus and plane trees have leaves again. His eyes shoot from his mother to the brown boxes, the elderly loiterer across the street, and he dashes back inside before his help can be enlisted. He wants nothing more to do with this.

* * * * *

Hollow-eyed young woman with a baseball glove she never broke in. Prematurely bald young man shuffling off to Buffalo. Children like short-lived particles in cloud chambers, known mainly in the tracks of their extinction—they were called. They had to go, but Henrietta went, on purpose, to that ugly, nameless, expensive little piece of real estate, believing she had made a choice when it was no choice at all. No wonder she is dissatisfied, that she is still seen around where she used to live, in pastry-shop windows or the Children's Reading Room at the library, just disappearing around corners, walking so straight and stiff in a red coat. She ought to have been buried with a stake through her heart. Had she been any kind of artist she would have known there is nothing artistic about death, which is the end of all stories.

In the Words of

TWO PEOPLE ARE IN A FIELD IN THE CATSKILLS. He is paint-
ing a watercolor. She is lying on a scratchy picnic-stained blanket, face down,
reading field guides, listening to the chipping sparrows burr in the scrub
oaks that stud the old pasture, a too loud towhee, some kind of woodpecker
booming beyond a stone wall that once kept the cows out of the woods.

She goes over to see what kind. Near the wall is a patch of spring beauty,
rose-veined, and white and lavender hepaticas. The field was filled with the
hot smell of strawberry flowers when they were here last May. They meant
to come back for the strawberries when they ripened. According to Euell
Gibbons, you can eat the roots of the spring beauty, boiled.

One, two, three red-tailed hawks spin over the valley, riding the ther-
mals, back and forth like prowl-car inspectors. She tracks them with the
binoculars he gave her for her birthday, which is the same as his.

He swishes a broad-tipped paintbrush around in one of two coffee
cans full of brook water, makes a wash, considers, and removes a fine-
pointed brush from the box she gave him to hold the tubes of paint—
alizarin crimson, burnt umber, forest green, Payne's gray.

The sky over the valley is an unpainterly cerulean.

Finally the painting is finished and they climb over another stone
wall out to the dirt road. The road's other side is wide open to the hills,

cleared land dropping away below them for miles. There are apple trees, buzzing with sparrows, above a white farmhouse, the closest landmark, and below that the increasingly flat perspective of stone-delineated fields, green-on-green polygons that recede in size and color like the paintings of Josef Albers. The fields fall to the valley crease, and on the other side the forest rises to join the sky.

The road is parallel to the valley; they begin to walk it without any discussion. Yellow-bellied sapsucker. Phoebes building a nest under a shelf of rock. A mushy spot in the road where water ran down from the mountainside (this is the watershed area); green shoots poking up in it. A brown thrasher asking everything twice, like a boring five-year-old. They walk close together, silent as painted people.

Words, after a while. She asks a question: "What is your day like?"

"Oh," he says, "I get up when I always did, go to bed at the usual time. It's important to make rules for yourself, and stick to them. . . . The trucks wake me," he adds, "and it takes me a long time to fall asleep again. I try to think about what to paint."

"Why don't you take something?"

"I'm through with props."

The road looks as though it must lead to a farmhouse. But it doesn't; they followed it once before, two birthdays ago. It leads deep into the woods and up a mountain. The trees as they walk get taller and older, blocking the valley view. An unkempt tangle of lilac which somebody planted, an unfamiliar fruit tree suggest some former habitation. (In the watery ditch last May bloomed forget-me-nots gone native out of some long-ago garden.)

"What do you have for breakfast?"

"Toast, coffee, juice."

"No more croissants?"

"Dr. Fellman told me I should lose ten pounds."

He looks thinner, almost ascetic; he has lost weight. Mostly around the face, a closening of skin to the bone structure, heightening the hawklike tenseness of his expression. There is a smudge of chemical green on one cheek.

"How do you spend the morning?"

"I'm taking a class at the New School. Just so I can have a place to paint with the right equipment, the right light. I paint there all morning." He considers a moment. "It takes a lot out of you, painting."

"Who do you eat lunch with?"

"Nobody. People in the class. Well, when I go uptown, fellows from the office if it isn't too late for them. Tuesdays, I have to lurk around the Bureaucracy."

"What do you do in the afternoon?"

"Usually I go home. Some afternoons I do another painting. Or answer letters and pay off the creditors. I try to take in the galleries; you can always learn from other people's successes and failures. Right now I'm hunting for a studio where I can paint all the time, and give classes."

"And give up the apartment?"

With surprise: "Oh, no. I'd never do that."

At this place in the road they saw, last time, a silly woodchuck trying to make a burrow in the hard dirt.

"Where have all the woodchucks gone?"

"I don't know." With better eyes than hers, he used to point out woodchucks spaced territorially along the Thomas E. Dewey Thruway, when they drove up to spend weekends at the Inn of the Four Seasons, or, in the words of the French, L'Auberge des Quatre Saisons. The seasons are deerslayers, skiers, fishermen, and swimmers.

"What do you do in the evening?"

"I would have been teaching that class at Brooklyn College. But only seven people signed up for it. You needed eight."

"Perhaps the word will have spread by next semester."

"Perhaps. It's hard," he admits, "to block in the time. The martinis get earlier and earlier. Five o'clock, then four-thirty, then four."

Except for one occasion, they haven't seen each other in six months. It was his idea for them to revisit this scene.

"Do you invite people to dinner?"

"Daphne has high blood pressure, and I haven't located another cook."

"Don't you get invited out?"

"Extra men are always being asked to dinner, thank you. Who wants to be *that*? Last night I ate at Barney and June's."

"How is Barney?"

"Barney's doctor told him his heart is six years older than the rest of him."

"How do you stand weekends? Saturday nights and Sunday afternoons?"

A slim sapling like a rod of copper, speckled white, some kind of fruit tree. Nothing here is in leaf or flower, not even the shadbush.

"I try to arrange things for weekends."

There are no more signs of a homestead, the road is well into the forest, wide enough for a jeep but redder and muddier and rutted, no longer going anywhere in particular, except up. They keep pausing, as birds shuttle back and forth across the road and she pursues them with the field glasses.

"Read any good books lately?"

"No."

"What about the theater?"

"I took in *Oh! Calcutta!* It was rotten."

"Haven't you kept up the subscriptions—Shakespeare, American Place?"

A shake of the head.

"Flicker, flicker," says a yellow-shafted one deep in the trees. It gets snowier the higher you go. Between the roots of the trees, gritty patches linger like white toes. And other things—a shotgun shell casing, a gold Ballantine beer can.

"Look—sportsmen," she says.

"People don't care what they throw away."

She sighs. "How long do you think it will be before the others discover this place?"

"They're probably on their way right now, Twig. It's going to be A-frames and Dairy Queens and beer cans and pay toilets right to the top of the mountain. People won't stop spreading. The trees are going to have to go."

From the throat of the woods the drumming of a large woodpecker, like the sound of an ax.

"But we need the forest. This is the watershed."

"They're going to flood this valley for a new reservoir. People won't stop breeding and spreading. In five years' time you won't recognize this place."

"What's the point of Earth Day, then? Zero Population Growth, recycling, anti-exhaust laws—" She stops when she sees he's not paying attention.

"Too late."

The valley is doomed. Water will lie upon the fields, the oriole-harboring orchards, the untidy, worthless back-country farms. This is the age of expenditure and success, expenditure and failure.

Climbing, a bit out of breath, into an earlier season: more snow and, on the north face of the rocks, frozen water like stopped fountains. They have never followed the road to the end.

"How far can we go?"

"We ought to begin to head back now. I've thought of some things to do to my painting."

"Let's get the car."

"Last time, if you will remember, we nearly got stuck to the hubcaps."

An enormous black bird explodes beside them, crosses the road stridently, and is absorbed by the trees before she has a chance to focus the binoculars.

"A pileated woodpecker!" She runs to the edge of the forest, searches for it. He looks at the sky, then at his uncle's heirloom watch.

"It was only a bluejay, Twig."

"Much larger than a jay. They're rare now, and I've never seen one. I need it for my life list."

But already he is walking away.

* * * * *

He is lighter, but his step is heavier, and his shoulder blades protrude in the chamois-cloth shirt that she ordered for him from L. L. Bean for Christmas. Like wings, but not the wings of a hawk.

Ask me a question, pessimistic sojourner. I'll tell you no lies.

"Don't you want to hear about me?"

Silence.

"Perhaps I talk too much; you don't talk enough. If only I could get inside your head for two seconds."

"In answer to what you said *first:* I'm aware that I'm not as communicative as some. So what? I'm so tired of always trying to please people."

"Wouldn't it be easier to look for a new job?"

"Listen, I'm trying to learn to enjoy my freedom. . . Freedom, I keep telling everybody, is for the birds."

"You are too hard on yourself always. Someone ought to tell you to be happy, for a change."

"I don't need anybody *else* to tell me anything. Look. I appreciate your intentions. Maybe you've gained a whole lot of insight. But I have to work things out my way. I just haven't got the future sketched in yet. Wait a few months."

"What about the cost of living?"

"The last time I paid my taxes I realized that I earned about the same amount as I get from the brokers. Well, I figured, I'm supposedly being paid a living wage, enough to support a family. So, since the only one I'm supporting is myself, I don't really need a salary, do I? In the words of Euclid, Q.E.D."

"What if we'd been married?"

"I don't want to talk about it."

"Did you ever really want to?"

"I *said*, I don't want to discuss it."

In silence the two of them descend, watching out for the wet spots, past the detritus of the hunters; the lilac bush that tells of a family that wrested a homestead out of the wilderness, cleared a field, fenced it in from the woods with the rocks from it, planted a garden and lilac, quit farming or died; the phoebes' nest of clay and debris. The forest reaches over the walls, sends out advance parties—alders in the marshy low places, scrub oaks in the dry.

The trees march down the hillside. But the people are flocking out of the cities. Having drunk up the snow, the troglodytes erupt into the valley and begin climbing the hill, irresistible in number, thrusting on and devouring everything along the way.

If only the trees could fight back: a leafy, shadowy army. There would be trees enough to take on every man, woman, and child. Hand to hand, branch to branch, who would win? Wood is harder than flesh. But flesh has hands, and metal, and the secret of fire.

Fully illuminated, the valley is completely still, except for the wind, and the birds; in the middle distance a few clouds are shaping up. A scarlet station wagon is parked alongside the pasture wall.

"Why didn't you buy a car with a convertible top?" The wind blew her hair into spaniel ears when, in the old car, they swooped over the top of the hill for the first time and discovered all this land, vacant of people for miles and miles, except for the dirt-poor farms tucked into side roads like this one, with forest, fields, and, at the bottom, the crooked valley stream.

Halfway down is a tiny cemetery on a little plateau, fenced in tidily like a rock garden, lonely as a moor. The state bird strolled bluely among the tombstones, mama and papa and four juveniles—a new species for her life list.

Pause. "Haven't you heard, Twig? The Great American Convertible as a species is extinct. Detroit doesn't make them anymore. The tops were always getting slashed."

"Let's drive down," she urges.

But he has returned to his easel; finds a need for another dark in the upper left, mixes burnt umber with forest green, wets the paper, strokes in color, which runs and feathers, dabs at it with a sponge, stands back. He has painted that tree over by the stone wall, lightning-struck, against a background of winter woods. On paper, it looks as if it were calling for help.

"It's good and strong. But I thought you had transcended your dead-tree period."

"I'm mostly abstract now, of course. You like it, Twig?"

* * * * *

"If you were a bird, what would you be?"

"An ostrich."

"What kind of landscape?"

"Flatness. The tundra. The veldt."

"Flower?"

"A lichen."

"That's not a flower."

"They survive."

"What weapon?"

"Anger."

He taught her to play that game when they drove for long distances at night and couldn't look at birds or landscapes. She said, "You," but the answer was "My father."

* * * * *

Only a month ago he had called. "Just checking in." Then he sighed deeply and said, "You might as well be among the first to know. They're letting people go down at the Lie Factory. Ten of us got the ax this morning."

"Who's us?"

"If you see a fellow selling apples at the corner of Madison and Forty-ninth, that'll be me. I'll save you a juicy one." A few minutes later, her phone rang again.

* * * * *

In an apartment, his, but she could tell you the number of floorboards in the living room, which seemed smaller: no rug. "The painters got more on my things than they did on the walls. I had to send it out for cleaning."

"You've moved the Mexican statue. I liked it under the skylight."

"The vandals smashed it."

He clutched her like a drowning person. "I'm going to miss the old place, I truly am. It's like losing your family. I've always had an office to go to. I even liked grinding out the fibs. Where am I going to go? What am I going to *do* all day?"

"You'll find another job."

"The old man used to hide behind the papers at breakfast so we couldn't see the look on his face—there was such emptiness in his eyes. I felt ashamed when I left for school, knowing he probably wished he could come along." He held on and on. "My mother was watching him once and she whispered, 'The poor little thing.' I didn't know who I wanted to choke, him or her."

Later he repeated several times, "I'm so frightened. I'm so afraid it's too late."

She told him it was not too late. She said anybody would be frightened. Quite a number of her friends were out of work. To be sure, they were living in hard times. Yet, with his abilities, his experience, she was sure he'd hit upon something. It was nothing to be ashamed of.

"Why did you come here? I'm so ashamed."

Then he remembered his plan. "I thought it all out while I was waiting for you to come." He'd go to the chief and ask if they couldn't keep him on as a consultant at, say, half of his present salary, and perhaps he could free-lance on the side. So that when business picked up— "I feel as though I'm too old to go looking for another job. I need my job. I need my family."

His heart thudding. She couldn't look at his face.

He whispered, "You shouldn't have come here. It is too terrible."

* * * * *

That was only a month ago. And now he has no family—a man who so desperately loathed weekends he'd go to the office on Saturdays, before he took up with painting and her, not necessarily in that order. His old hat is jammed down over his forehead; his voice drops at the end of every sentence, angry, abrupt, and hollow. Every day is a weekend now.

Something like a bad cold inundates her eyes, her throat. Sorrow? Pity? No, she refuses to savage him with her pity. He is not a poor little thing. *They* are not poor little things.

Last week she opened a book and a picture floated onto the bed, a photograph of him, grinning at the camera and slightly out of focus. His hair was black; a piece of it fell over one eye. He looked as if he were about to ask a question.

Once he said, "I want to die," and she believed he would die without her. Whom does he talk to now about his paintings and the household gods, rage, futility, loneliness, anxiety, and despair? After a martini or two he sometimes would pat her knee: "Twig. You're not so bad. There's a lot going on behind that smiling face. You've wisdom enough for both of us, if we just knew how to tap it." Eyes across the valley, where the water-bearing cumuli are streaming, receding like years, like five years.

Five years ago she was drowning and called out to him. And he saved her; he pulled her in, gave her artificial respiration, dried her off, permitted her to continue. How did she know he couldn't swim either? Cravenly she attacked his resources, insisting that he flourish, take an interest; she encouraged him to paint, which he is doing full time now, morning, noon, and night, though the martinis get earlier and earlier and he wakes at three in the morning.

Oh dear, she filled his days but she could not add to them. Ultimately he was exhausted. He betrayed her: he got old—

Inclining always, anyway, toward death, away from life, stubbornly chopping at the foundations. At a distance she must follow him, strolling toward death in his L. L. Bean shirt and his old hat. Like a tortoise she had, a dry-land creature with a yen for streams and rivers; put him down near the bank and he struck out at once for the water. It whirled him away upside down in his shell, like a rudderless boat. No matter how you turned him around, he swerved back, ineluctably heading for the torrent. She held him back for a while but she couldn't turn him around, he was so eager to get away, perhaps more eager than ever.

* * * * *

In the watershed region two people stand overlooking a lit valley, watching the clouds that move up from the ocean like buckets, dropping water that runs through leaves and tree roots down the slopes into trout streams with Indian names, streams that feed into the reservoir, to flow through the aqueduct pipes for a hundred miles to rise in the dirty, thirsty city where they live. In the rich and airy landscape she gropes for a way out of sorrow, can find none.

"Oh, why did we live together so long? What was the point?"

Looking down at the valley soon to be drowned, he replies finally, remotely, without tenderness, "Don't ask me, Twig."

In the words of W. H. Auden, "Thousands have lived without love, not one without water."

THE LISTS OF THE PAST

The Stories of the House

Saturday 8/30/69

(1) Cut Grass South Side

(2) Rake Turnaround

(3) Prune

    a—Garage Maple

    b— " Mulberry

    c—Front "

(4) Choking Pine?

(5) Front Taxus

(6) Side Apple Tree

(7) Move Cut Stuff from Side

(8) Pickets?

(9) Mirror?

1, 2, 4, and 9 have been excised from this list of chores with a horizontal stroke; 9, in addition, with a neat tick mark. The following day,

Sunday 8/31

he has more plans:

Stain Desk

(1) Front Porch Stuff
(2) Apple Tree
(3) Maple Tree
(4) Chair
(5) TRH Book Case
    Cut Out
(6) Drug Stuff
(7) Cokes   (8) Lettuce

Evidently, the desk was stained, front porch cleaned up, maple and apple pruned. Cokes, drug stuff, lettuce bought. Lettuce bought? No, lettuce weeded, or picked, because this is an outdoorsman's list, a suburban gardener's, and lettuce, given its head, by August is almost a nuisance vegetable.

The lists are in a clipboard on a cellar workbench totally marred by nail holes, rust, paint, glue, hammer gouges, and cigarette burns, and are written on all kinds of paper: lined tablet, milk-order forms, old envelopes, the backs of grocery bills. Dampness and dirt have weathered the lists, softened the penciled admonitions, some of which are for others:

Myron—Paint New Window.

Or:

Water Hyacinths
C—Feed Birds
Plant Bulbs?

The latter an afterthought, boxed in with red pencil at the top of a more ambitious schedule—his or Myron's?

(1) Vacuum and Scrub around Furnace

(2) Tighten Storm Windows

    a—Study

    b—all others

(3) Wash Window Landing—chamois

    a—Inside

    b—Outside?

    3a—Move Study Furniture

(4) Polish Brass Work

(5) Wash Butlers Pantry Doors

(6) Turn Geraniums

(7) Xmas Stuff to 3rd Floor

(8) Drain Boiler

Nos. 1, 3, 7, and 8 crossed off; along the bottom, in another handwriting, the message *See you in two weeks.*

Such a lot of things for him to do, that have to be done, inside and outside. If he (or Myron) isn't trimming cedars, he's topping 2 hemlocks, trimming All Bushes by House, weeding, feeding roses, trimming cedars (jobs move through the lists till they're crossed out, or make comebacks). The house demands perpetual care. Washing, painting, seasonal chores, restless furniture. Red armchair ever on the gad: 2nd Floor to Maid's Room, to basement, Garage Loft. He listens to the sounds of the house at night, roof cricking in the January freeze—loose shingle? What is that noise in the walls, like water leaking from a pipe, oozing down through the insulation to drip through the new paint on my living-room ceiling? Call Electrician reg. Hissing Sound. Oven Pilot Light. Clean up Garden. Paint Garage Cable. Kill Crab.

Why, he works like a slave.

* * * * *

Beside Xmas stuff on 3rd Floor, in a roomy closet, a carton of photographs at least eighteen inches deep. Here, in the middle of the collection, a young man leans on an ax, foot on a tree stump, somewhere along the Appalachian Trail, chin thrust toward the camera—a man who simply has cut down a tree. Here the same young man is again (among ancestors, collaterals, peers, strangers, friends, a German wedding party circa 1910), a father looking at a baby in a playpen—and a different, cruder house, with an open porch that will become a sunroom, a wilderness of lawn, and only some hollyhocks to adumbrate a garden. Here are hundreds of other people, a cast of thousands. Babies. Grandpas. Husbands and wives. Youngsters. So many children—still, for once, squinting, cartwheeling, posing, making their First Communion, in knickers, lace dresses, pinafores, bathing suits, gingham, corduroy, cotton, Dacron; children dead for ages, children with their children. Six little boys arranged in birth order (second from the right, in hand-me-down corduroy, serious, two thousand miles away). People as found in the viewfinders of dozens of cameras, dating back to the invention of film, amid all sorts of views (they travel a lot) or at home, where interiors are curiously the same. Look-alikes and strangers, dear ones and dull—interesting if you got to know them, maybe, but by and large, unintroduced like guests at a bad party, no livelier than the leaves that lie raked for his compost heap. He isn't here, and, downstairs, a doorbell is ringing.

* * * * *

He is, of course, working in the garden. In *one* of the gardens. The mirror garden, divided crescents, reverse images. (Myron's dark shoulders disappear around the side of the house, steering the power mower, diminishing whir.)

He is moving the lawn sprinkler, the rainbow-catcher, to refreshen the sweet William, the columbine, Turk's-cap lilies, phlox—a gaudy perennial garden, favoring the reds and oranges, vivid against the green of the rose-of-Sharon hedge, whose purple trumpets are just beginning to blow. Two thorny climbing roses bridge the arch that leads to the bottom of the lawn, the apple trees, rose and vegetable gardens. He hasn't bothered to turn off the water, because he likes its cold surprise on his freckled back (as the day heats up he will shed most of the clothes he began in, ending up clad merely in unself-conscious modesty and bathing trunks). "Whew." Panting, he straightens, grabs a bandanna handkerchief from a stone bench under the silver maple, smiles. "Well, hello."

"Aren't you afraid you'll get sunstroke?"

"They really needed that. Do you know we've had practically *no* rain this August!"

In spite of the dry spell, the lawn has maintained its green, the garden its hues, phlox and sweet William are lustrous under their shower bath. It is a radiant, a glistery day. The water evokes, as well as color, fragrance: newly cut grass. Whiff of sweet William and, from the rose garden, roses. He turns, contemplates the green circle of lawn, with the silver maple in the center, the terrace, the shuttered Victorian house. "I've got to do something about those rhododendrons," he says, jabbing a finger at their unkempt foliage. "The terrace needs a new coat of paint." However, he appears satisfied with the progress he and Myron are making, arresting the tendency of things to wear down and out according to the well-known Second Law of Thermodynamics. Swish swish of the sprinkler on the soft petals of flowers.

"*Ben! Lunchtime!*"

The house looks imposing even from its back, the kitchen side. Three stories tall: many gables, many windows, and chimneys, shingles recently painted light, or cactus, green, veranda on two and a half sides, and on this one a glass porch, where there can be seen more plants. The house was built before the Civil War. Part of it, anyway. Only a study of the tattered blueprints rolled up on his closet shelf could show you which part; it has been through a lot of architectural fooling around. The basement and the east lower two stories for sure. There is a secret crawl space under the veranda. The original owners were Abolitionists, and it is said the house was a stop on the Underground Railroad.

It was built as the guest cottage on an estate, when the village was all the grounds of a manor, and the street outside a drive, an alley to the edge of the Sound. Then it became a summer house, when this was a summer town, a refuge for well-off city people, and the town seemed farther from the city than it does now, though easily accessible by train. There are many houses of this sort in the vicinity. High-ceilinged structures designed to accommodate large families, before air conditioning (or birth control), when labor was cheap and taste eclectic; fake turrets, widow's walks, and gingerbread jigsaw work abound—with service bells and fireplaces in every room. When there were plenty of servants to answer the bells, to open the windows to the breezes from the Sound at night, and draw the curtains in the morning. Not many others, though, have lawns front and back, three gardens, two compost heaps, and an unattached garage that used to hold carriages.

During the Depression the title passed to a bank. When he bought it, just before the Second World War, there were only two other houses on the block, and from where he is standing, under the maple, he could see over a tennis court and a field clear to the river.

"Ben! Time for lunch!"

There are more roses, and a cutting garden, tulips lying low till next spring, along the east foundations of the house, but no flowers in front, the dark, north-facing side. Just the rhododendrons growing up to each side of the veranda steps, and the bush in front of them, where two nearly invisible paths lead to the wide formal lawn, sloping down to the street, nearly a quarter of an acre. Myron is mowing it now.

The front lawn, though well tended, is hardly used except by child trespassers, who are always welcome, and the unprosecutable starlings and robins. This yard is almost a separate lot, large enough to be zoned for construction, though fortunately they never needed to sell or build on it. A hedge of rhododendron mixed with evergreen shrubbery nearly conceals the lower stories of the house from the sidewalk. Since the garage is in back, the occupants, and even most visitors, generally enter the house through the kitchen door.

Only when you are driving up the long, graveled approach or stand at the foot of the lawn can you really see the columned neo-antebellum façade, with the covered double-decker veranda, and appreciate what the architectural tinkerers had in mind. From this angle, lawn, pillars, the dark hemlocks that shield it from its neighbor on the far side of the drive, the great maples and elms—all majestically proportionate, the right scale. The house looks grand, shaded, serene.

"*Ben!*"

* * * * *

Peace came to the village, followed by the bulldozer. The great gardens, lawns, tennis and croquet courts shrank, diminished in number, disappeared; one-story buildings uniformly replaced the vacant lots and orchards, mushroomed and filled in the spaces around the old houses to the limits of growth. The village, though three times as large as before, has really stopped growing and is peaceful again, an orderly town, observing the limits. No one but a stranger would think of driving faster than the twenty-five m.p.h. ordained. (Last week, a couple of house-hunters swerved to dodge a bicycle being ridden by a child reading a comic book and ran over the Sanders' Weimaraner, at large and violating the leash laws.)

Though empty houses are snapped up at once, it's more like a village again. Most people have lived here long enough to be able to nod to one another on the train, at church or temple, and to belong to the ambulance corps of the volunteer fire department, serve on the library committee, join any of three beach clubs (except for the Jews). Their children—and sometimes their grandchildren—move into the split-level if they can't afford the Victorian. They sit elbow-to-blanket on the tiny beaches, where every year winter washes away the sand that is barged in every spring from Long Island.

Evenings, screen doors bang behind children rushing out to meet each other for hide-and-seek, giant steps, dead dog, red light. Teen-agers play radios by the diminutive but authentic coves and promontories of the public park—which are said to have sheltered pirates and smugglers, and did harbor deer, and now a strange melanistic race of gray squirrels—and get caught smoking contraband substances by the watchful police force of two. Their parents entertain with more traditional fare, outdoor cookouts, the smell of barbecue smoke in the air, the chime of cocktail glasses and rising voices.

Right now you would think they had all gone down to the water—to the park or to the beaches to watch their children or boats. A poor day for sailing, though, windless and still. In the garden, only the sound of the mower and the lawn sprinkler, and footfalls on the hollow veranda, where a blond lady in harlequin glasses is showing a young couple up the steps that strangers use.

From a becalmed sailboat, the village shimmers like a road mirage, looks almost as green as it might have to its European discoverers several centuries ago.

"Ben, lunch is ready! Come out of the garden!"

He double-checks to make sure it can do without him for the next minute and a half, and goes in through the kitchen to draw a glass of water from a faucet in the butler's pantry.

* * * * *

Over the polished-copper pantry sink is the bell box; when a bell upstairs or down is pressed, a white card drops with a click behind the glass face to tell which room you are ringing from. Living Room. Parlor. Master Bedroom. *Front Door.*

He fixed it up to amuse the grandchildren. But the wiring in the walls, the nerves of the house, is fully modern, functioning well even with all five air-conditioners going at once.

Stand on the gray veranda, a little to the left of the front door, and you can look clear through the house: through living room, dining room, into the solarium, and through that to the lawn and the mirror garden and the rose-of-Sharon arch, down to the hedge where the cardinal nests (three broods this year), to the boy-face fountain and the dog's gravestone and the cemetery the neighborhood children made, stone specks among ivy, under the cedars that so constantly have to be trimmed.

Now come in through the front door. Inside, you will see that here at least he hasn't right now to work so hard. The inside of the house is tidy as a tomb. It is only last year, after all, that the painters took away their buckets and drop cloths, and they got the decorator's bill. The bad patch in the living-room ceiling where the water leaked (but the plumbing, the guts of the house, is really quite sound, all copper) has been replastered. Upstairs and down, the screens over the windows (the eyes of the house) are mended and fast, not even to be thought about until late September, when they will be replaced by storm windows, ever in need of tightening.

The entrance-hall mirror reflects the stained-glass Art Nouveau fanlight over the front door; beneath the mirror, in the fireplace, a music box inlaid with Swiss scenes—one of many he discovered and repaired. Listen a minute. The spiny cylinder disturbs the comb's teeth, which move up and down like tiny piano keys, playing operatic melodies. *Martha.* " 'Tis the Last Rose of Summer." On your left is the round green parlor, full of breakables, the glass doves and fragile glass-topped bibelot table and the white-and-gold Bavarian-china breakfast set, an anniversary present. Women took tea there, pressed the mother-of-pearl bell button for the butler, when there were butlers to answer the bell.

Now the high-ceilinged living room, really as big as two rooms. No ashes in the big fireplace with the Spanish marble mantelpiece, or in the ashtrays; the fat silk cushions on the chairs are plumped up. Their very best furniture, winnowed through the years, safe from defacement now the children are grown up. Curly-backed Victorian sofa they discovered right after they were married, when antique shopping was cheaper. He dickered the proprietor down, bought it for a song. There's the eighteenth-century chest they bought in Ireland. The brown velvet love seat, polished to a patina by the seats of non-Victorian children using it for a slide.

The floorboards in the dining room waxed to a mirror finish; likewise the dining-room table, with the chairs from an English jury room. He spent a winter sanding it, and varnished it seven times.

Up the staircase a girl would be proud to throw her bouquet from, pausing on the landing to admire the wide window that admits whatever light can get through the hemlocks, back-lighting the garden-colored paperweights and vases on the glass shelves. Listen to the other music boxes, large and small, classical and romantic and schmaltz, Mozart and Strauss, drums and castanets, *sostenuto, andante.* Upstairs hallway. Four bedrooms, three baths, a washer should take care of that leaky faucet some rainy day, plenty of room for a growing family.

From the front bedrooms, French doors open onto the second story of the covered veranda. (Children have skated there in wet weather in spite of the ordinances.) More rooms, and closets, some of them room-size, in the finished third floor; the attic. The memory of the house. And its gizzard, too, catchall for the things that don't go anywhere else. Last Xmas. Red armchair, broken paperback books, old clothes, old toys. Boxes labeled according to their contents or destination: 3rd Floor, Misc. Silver, Apoth. Jars, Junk. It is not very tidy. It is a mess, as a matter of fact. Someone has been looking for things, or packing. However, you might as well look at the big fan that sucks up the hot air and helps keep the house cool at night, the air space that insulates and cuts way down on the air-conditioning bill, the lungs, so the house can breathe and the owners sleep soundly. Look out on the trees—the trees have grown high, even after all that building. From the dormer casement windows above the tree line all you see is waves of dark August leaves, and a glimpse of blue water.

Up here, too, is another domicile, alter ego of the real one, the doll house. The children have failed to replace the front, detachable wall. The house stands open like a bombstruck mansion.

He made the model, working, by necessity, winter evenings in the basement, where his tools are, the heart of the house, with its furnace hissing, the smell of glue and solder. He built it as a birthday present for one daughter while the other helped him, watching mostly, as he turned the fine mahogany banister (just like the one that in the real house weaves from the second floor) and set in the tiny, perfect spokes. It is built exactly to scale: an inch to a foot. If a six-inch family man moved in, he would find it in working order (except for the plumbing)—light switches in every room to turn on and off, shutters that open and shut— made with a fidelity to detail so obsessive that even the blind room at the top of the stairs has a door that a doll-mother could walk through carrying linen to change the bed in the lace-curtained master bedroom.

Red lights in the fireplaces to simulate fires; lights even for the attic (unfinished), where Xmas stuff is stored, a plastic tree and chips of wood covered with red and gold foil to put under it. He scored the Plexiglas crescent attic windows with a nail, in a haze of blue Lucky Strike smoke, sitting down every so often to run his fingers over the piano keys. Next year, for the other daughter, he created an ell.

Living room, dining room, turkey on the sideboard, the rest of the dinner in the kitchen, icebox full of synthetic goodies. No cellar, of course, or a garden—it stands on a plywood platform with turnaround and shade trees and ornamental shrubs. The piano in the doll house plays "Happy Birthday." The doorbells ring, front and back. He ordered expensive furniture from a hundred-page catalogue, papered the walls with Paisley and florets, book-lining paper. They stocked it with a doll family that kept on growing: a father, a mother, boy and girl twins, a baby, a nurse, and a uniformed maid to answer the door.

And the real little girls played with it, in it. A leg broke off the Hepplewhite sofa. The miniature *New York Times* was read to bits. The music-box workings of the piano faltered. The imitation food disappeared, though it was never consumed; dust darkened the white curtains and the maid was helpless to prevent it. And the neighborhood children, and now the grandchildren, innocently fascinated by its smallness, oblivious to its beauty. Their small hands buzz the doorbell, turn the lights (radio tubes) on and off, leaving them on all night. They have recently been playing Moving Man, with a dump truck, which is at the back door, and the living-room furniture (what remains of it) out on the fake lawn; and of the dolls only the wife is left.

* * * * *

Down the uncarpeted flight to the second-floor landing, and on down the steep back stairs to the big kitchen. The stomach of the house. The dinette looks out over the garden; the dishwasher's old but has never given much trouble, though the Disposal has swallowed a spoon and not yet digested it. But that's all right, since he sees to it that the tea leaves and coffee grounds, organic waste, are kept out for the mulch pile.

No, that is not a bearing wall, and you could break through the dinette into the solarium to convert the family room so many young families seem to need. This door opens onto the steps to the basement, and outside there's a ground-level alternative entrance, the old-fashioned canted cellar doors opening outward, for toddlers to creep up and slide down.

* * * * *

Pick up the wrought-iron filigree key from the hook by the kitchen door, walk outside, and around up the gray veranda steps near the solarium. Do you see this chest, painted gray to match the porch? The painters were surprised when they tried to move it. Because it is a trick. It has a hinged top, and is unlocked with the old-fashioned key, and when the lid is thrown back it reveals a short steep flight of steps, with a rope banister, leading to the very bottom part of the house. At the foot of the steps there is a door on each side. One opens into the basement proper, the other into a chamber hollowed out in the dirt foundation under the veranda, deep enough for a man to stand upright in, wide enough to live in if you had to.

The foundation, on the far side, is an eighteen-inch ledge of rock; though the floor is dirt, even in hurricane weather it stays dry—this is one of the driest basements in town.

Now through the other door, to the basement itself, where he worked on the doll house and other projects, with whatever energy remained after the five-fifty-seven commute, builder as well as breadwinner— finishing antique furniture, never finishing that old organ over there by the whitewashed wall.

Here he is, taking a break from yard work to oblige the neighbor children, who want to listen to him play. In the music corner, with a cumbersome record player of the fifties and an old Victrola where the little dog no longer barks, the bookshelf full of 78-r.p.m. jazz records, the upright piano, a Steinway. The voice of the house.

He switches on the brass standing lamp, lights a cigarette, puts it in the ashtray on top of the piano beside the Fake Book, swings into an old-time medley. "Do you know what it means, to miss Noo Orleans? Missed the Saturday dance. Got as far as the door. Thought they'd ask me *about* you; don't get around much anymore. Liza, Liza, dee da da. I'll be down to getcha in a taxi, Honey, you better be ready about half past eight . . ." and their favorite, the Alligator Crawl. Hepcat Rumble. But he has to feed his roses now, do the compost heap behind the hedge a good turn. The black squirrel is burying a nut in the animal graveyard his friends the children made. The roses have to be cut or they will go to seed and cease to flower. He has to get back to his cabbage kingdom.

* * * * *

Footsteps on the porch, lantern bobbing, extinguished. Click, the key finds the lock, creak, the top of the false chest is thrown back, the side panel released. A mist from the water hides the moon, making their passage up from the beach safer though harder: white man in dark trousers, leather boots, sweating in the breathless August heat, black man wearing all that he owns, a lent white shirt open at the neck, tattered pants, vaguely luminous. Tomorrow they'll give him boots for his travel-torn feet.

Escort and his charge feel for the footholds, descend. Open the door to the hiding hole. Fumble for the candle, in a holder set into the wall. A guttering orange light discloses the chamber, provisioned with pallet, commode, a covered basket, doorway so low that the black man must duck his head. "Now, there's food in that basket. Remember your instructions. Tomorrow night after sunset"—but no window to tell when sunset will be—"three knocks, and they'll be dressed in gray. Try to move around as little as possible."

Mute with fear and fatigue, the black man tries to speak, can only nod his head.

The door closes, the bolt is slid back, footsteps over his head, through the leaves, gone. Back to the beached dory, to row with a faint swish of oars out to the other boat that ferried them here across the water. Amos the slave, a free man now, listens for the sounds of the house, but the occupants sleep, oblivious to the errand that has just been completed. Should anyone ask, they have heard nothing.

Tomorrow when the sun has gone down, two men in gray, wide hat brims partially shielding their faces, are to lead him through the woods to a tunnel, stumbling together through the fetid passage to another cellar, up the secret stairs, to the night air. A coach will be waiting. Up the Boston Post Road, dressed as a woman, many changes, many houses— Canada! Amos the free man shivers in the humid compartment, too tired even to taste what's in the basket, watching the flame diminish, expiring, waiting for darkness. When it comes he must not cry out. He thinks of Georgia, of the North Star, his children, and shuts his eyes. They had not thought to leave him candles enough for his vigil.

The candle goes out.

Who is at the door? Why is the furniture out on the lawn? What is he doing beside the compost heap, standing so still and reading the new inscription the children have written on the wooden pedestal in the center of the animal cemetery? Where are they all driving away to without looking back? When will he come out of the garden? And walk through the French doors of the solarium, into the house, with his hands full of Bibb lettuce, and roses—Helen Traubel, Sterling Silver, five kinds of Peace.

"Eighteen Down"

"WHAT TIME IS IT?" asks a woman in a bed jacket, waking in her lightproof bedroom one May morning.

"Nine-thirty." Her daughter stands over the bed. "Mother, please let me open the curtains. It's an outstanding day."

"That late! I must have fallen off, then. Did you say half past nine?"

The younger woman moves to the French doors, pulls the cord to draw aside heavy satin draperies, snaps up the shades, swings open the doors, admitting light and weather: the day is as reported, though chilly—it has been a backward month. She steps out onto the second-story balcony. The budding boughs are leafless but the grass green again; starlings stroll on the wide lawn among the hemlock cones like a convention of under-takers. By the side of the house, the magnolias have fully bloomed and are dropping their petals like pink shells on the driveway gravel.

She shivers (it's really too cold still to be outside without a sweater) and goes in to ask, "Could I poach you an egg?"

"Oh, please don't bother," says the mother. "Close the doors? I'm freezing. But you could bring me a cup of coffee."

Her daughter starts downstairs.

"Cornelia! Milk toast. Do you know how to make milk toast? I used to fix it for you when you were sick. A slice of Pepperidge Farm white bread, toasted, and buttered on both sides. Heat the milk just to scalding, don't let the skin come . . . Oh, darling!" she calls.

Cornelia pauses on the landing.

"Is the *Times* here yet? I'd like to do the puzzle."

* * * * *

"Please close the curtains, dear. The light hurts my eyes." Now the mother is sitting up in bed, reading glasses sliding down her nose, *New York Times* folded back to the crossword puzzle. On a shelf at her left hand is a white telephone. On the other side of the bed, a night table just large enough to hold an ashtray, water glass, lamp, alarm clock. A wicker standing-tray, with a bowl containing a half-eaten island of toast floating in gold-flecked milk, has been pushed to the foot of the bed.

The daughter picks up the tray and sets it on the floor. She pulls up a little boudoir chair, closes the curtains, sits upright, feet on the carpet, palms on her lap.

"What's a five-letter word for 'lively'?"

" 'Alert'?"

"No, that doesn't fit." The mother bites her lip, glances at the telephone. "What time is it?"

"Just after ten. I'm going out to see the garden. If you need me, holler."

"It's a mess. It makes me sick to look at it. I'm all right. I'm just going to lie here and work this puzzle. 'Quick'!" She fills in the word.

It's warmer in back of the house, the south side, where the gardens are. Not much green yet in the vegetable garden, untended, stony. Cornelia kneels by the place where the perennials aren't blooming yet, and parts the ragged dark evergreen ground cover at the border. Green shoots peep up underneath.

The rosebushes look terrible, haggard after a long winter's night on the town—a jungle, in fact, of wildly unchecked new growth which ought long since to have been pruned back. Eight new ones have been recently planted, naked little canes with bracelet name tags. She picks up a metal tag that has fallen from one of the new bushes: *Helen Traubel. Sexual reproduction of this plant without license is strictly prohibited. . . .* A trowel has been thrown down beside it in the grass, as if whoever put the roses in was planning to return in a minute. Rusting. She takes the trowel into the garage and goes back into the house.

The bedroom even darker by contrast with out-of-doors, yellowly lit and foggy with cigarette smoke. In her absence, the mother has pulled the shades back down, closed the draperies again and pinned them to the shades with a hatpin. Cornelia carries the tray out into the hall. "Did anybody call?"

"Oh, I'm sure it's too early to hear anything yet."

"How are you doing with the puzzle?"

"I'm having difficulty with this section here."

"Let's see. 'Patio-chair material.' 'Tartan'? I think you've got the letters wrong; it must be 'rattan.' 'Empty' is 'inane.' I've no idea what 'an Arabian drink' is. The garden's a sorry sight, all right." They sit awhile without speaking, Cornelia on the boudoir chair, her mother propped against the pillows, No. 2 Venus pencil poised over the puzzle but not moving.

"What time is it?"

"I don't know. Come outside," begs the daughter. "Get up. Move around. It's easier when you keep busy."

"I *am* keeping busy. I'm smoking and doing a crossword puzzle. Why don't you do something helpful? Go uptown for me."

"What do you want?"

"Well, what do we need? Damn it, he's been doing all the shopping. Since you're going: butter, we must be almost out of butter."

"Vegetables?"

"Pick up some frozen. Any kind, doesn't matter. String beans, peas. Better get some more cigarettes, too." The ashtray on the night table is running over with the wrinkled stumps of half-smoked Kents. "Do you remember Gristede's? They'll know who we are. Tell them to charge it to us."

* * * * *

The traffic in the shopping section of the small village is hectic—mostly women driving alone to pick up their school-children or groceries, on the way from the hairdresser, bumper-to-bumper on the Boston Post Road. Nobody recognizes her at Gristede's as she collects the family order.

She drops in at a garden store. The fire whistle blasts: Noon. Children who haven't been picked up are on their way home from the two schools, public and parochial, the Catholics in uniform—absentmindedly reckless on bikes, on foot, crossing the streets wherever they feel like it. A big-breasted crossing guard in a blue uniform smiles pleasantly as she holds up a stream of automobiles. Nobody honks. At the corners, tulip-yellow signs hinged across the middle have opened out from the tree trunks: Stop. Children Cross Walk. Watch out for children, riding home along magnolia-puddled sidewalks by the street that leads to the Sound.

The bed has been made and the mother is reclining on it, in a lacy beige dressing gown, staring at the telephone. "No word yet. We should be hearing by now."

"Shall we call the hospital?"

"Oh no, what would *they* know? What time is it?"

Half past May.

The telephone rings. The mother puts out her left hand for the receiver. "Oh. Hello, Alice. No, not a thing. It was supposed to be all over by now. I don't know what's taking so long."

"Oh, I'm sure it will."

"Well, Finley said there was no point being at the hospital, waiting around. He won't wake up for hours."

"Yes, Intensive Care."

"Sweet of you. But Cornelia's here with me."

"I'll call you the *minute* I hear. How is Nan's baby?"

"Oh, that's good news," she chuckles, and hangs up.

"Those poor children. You remember Nan had another baby, Cornelia? Her husband is out of a job and they just put a down payment on a house in Valhalla and the third baby turned out to be Rh-negative; it was touch and go for a while, but now the baby's okay. It seems terribly stuffy in here. Do you feel hot?" There are beads of sweat on her forehead. "What was the weather report?"

"Call and find out."

"It would tie up the phone. Did it rain last night? Did you see any rain in the rain gauge? He'd like to know."

Her hand moves instinctively toward the receiver; she draws it back, hesitates, shrugs, picks up the whole thing, and rests it beside her on the bedspread like a white kitten. With a hand that is lightly freckled, lightly trembling, she dials anyway. W. E. 6. 1. 2. 1. 2. The Weather Bureau.

Cornelia goes downstairs at last with the breakfast tray, setting it on the table in the downstairs hall in order to pull open the door to the kitchen. In the Canton bowl on the marble top lies a toy that has evidently strayed from a doll house—a toy woman in a rumpled frock ballooning over old-fashioned white underpants, flung on her back, head toward the bottom of the bowl, painted high-heeled shoes kicking at the sides, movable arms thrown behind her painted coiffure as if she were screaming.

Regarding the roses: their looks haven't improved any since she last saw them—beauties who've let themselves go, mass of snarls. Several tenths of an inch of rain have fallen on the garden and its hydrometer, an inverted plastic wedge. From out in the garden the ring of the telephone can be heard.

* * * * *

The mother, on the phone again, shakes her head negatively. "Has André got back from Bermuda?" ("I'm talking to the hairdresser," she mouths.)

"If he could squeeze me in."

"Tomorrow would be dandy. My husband can't drive me. He's having an operation, but I'll manage somehow. I can take a cab."

"Mother, I'll drive you, for heaven's sake."

"Oh, we're sure everything will be all right. Tomorrow at eleven, then. Bye." The older woman hangs up and says, uncertainly, "I'm scandalously overdue for a permanent." Gray curly wisps stick to her forehead; she pushes at the hairline with the heel of her hand. "I haven't even combed it this morning. I must be a sight to frighten children and dogs."

"I thought I heard the telephone ring in the garden."

"That was Mona. She didn't want to hold up the line, but *she* couldn't figure out eighteen down, either. It's a long one. Tear of the number thirteen.' "

"How many letters?"

"Seventeen."

" 'Triskaidekaphobia.' " Cornelia spells it. Her mother fills in the letters carefully.

"I think you're right. It fits. Aren't you clever! What time is it?"

Her daughter adjusts the clock on the bedside table so that her mother can see it better.

"Really, I should comb my hair at least."

"You look all right."

"It is like that poem about soldiers combing their hair before a battle. What is it? *You* must remember. A battle they were sure to lose, but they went in in their best clothes."

"The Spartans. The Spartans at Thermopylae. Look it up, it must be in the Bartlett's." In the bookcase beside the mother's bed is a handy reference library—Roget, Webster, 1922 guide to the Greek myths—for when crosswords are truly stymieing.

The clock face finally catches the mother's attention. "That clock must be fast. I think I'll call MEridian 7"—putting down the pencil. The telephone rings.

"Oh, hello, Polly. Not a peep yet."

"Of course not, it's nice to hear your voice."

"Just lying here doing a crossword puzzle with Cornelia. Imagine, a minute ago I was making an appointment to have André do my hair! We were trying to think of that poem about the Spartans arranging their hair before the battle of Thermopylae, you know, dressing up for disaster."

"The oddest things."

"I'm sure it will but I wish that damn hospital would call. Heard anything about Ronnie's draft deferment?"

"He's going to *what?*"

"Oh my, yes, the minute we hear."

Hanging up, she explains to her daughter, "Poor Ronald's number 19 in the draft lottery. He's decided to diet down to below the permissible weight limit, which means he has to lose fifty pounds. He says it's either that or Canada. Polly thinks he knows what he's doing. Didn't you used to babysit for him, Cornelia?"

"He was always pestering me with questions. Like could he have a chocolate-éclair Good Humor. Does he need a job this summer? Maybe he could help out in the gardens."

"Not if he's fasting," says her mother, dryly. She looks at the puzzle, a blur, at the clock, blur. Lighting a cigarette. "Wouldn't you know, now I've mislaid my glasses. What time is it?"

"I can't tell from here. Lunchtime? Let me make you a sandwich," she offers. "Wouldn't you like a bite to eat now?"

"Here they are, in the editorial section. One o'clock. Well. I believe I'll spruce up. Could you bring me a brush, a mirror?" The Spartans on the something rock—

Pale face bobs in the mirror she holds at arm's length. Brushing the hair back from the forehead, puffing the sides into shape. "Heavens, how gray I am." The Spartans on the sea-wet rock—

The telephone rings.

Sat down and combed their hair.

Gardening for Pleasure

"CUT ABOVE AN OUTWARD-FACING BUD." But which bud is leaf, which is flower? Cornelia is about to start pruning the roses. Finally. That is, she is looking them over.

It has been a late spring, and a damn cold May so far, which has helped keep weeds out of the garden, or gardens. The rose beds are two fairly sizable strips, an I and an L, separated by a grassy path, for kneeling and working. Beyond them, the region for vegetables, currently a slough too disreputable and vast even to contemplate. The rosebushes are at least neatly mulched with buckwheat hulls. Everything above the roots is disorder; the bushes have riotously thrown out hundreds of shoots every which way, covered with shiny reddish leaves. These ought to have been shorn by April, according to the book. Leave out all but the essential—three good, healthy canes from which will evolve Y-shaped, branches clustered with roses, for summer flower arrangements.

Water runs down Cornelia's face. (It's also been a rainy spring.) She goes in by the back, or garden, door of the garage.

Besides the car, a kingly green Oldsmobile, the garage is full of garden equipment: bags of fertilizer, a hand mower, a power mower, spades and rakes, old bushel baskets, seedlings, outdoor chairs, bird chow, seven pairs of pruning shears, a rubber kneeling mat. A beat-up little three-legged table with more clutter, clippers, a memorandum or list:

TUESDAY

Garden

(1) Prune Beach Ave Walk

(a) Stake Tomatoes

(b) Block Out Onions or Pull all Weeds

(c) Roses—1) Feed all in bed & gardens

2) Debud & prune

(d) Phlox—Tie

(e) Azaleas—Feed Hollytone

Walk—Water in ＂

—Buckwheat Hulls

(f) Other Azaleas Feed

(g) Prune Bushes by Garbage & Kitchen Door

(h) Compost from N.W. Corner

(i) Start new Compost Heap in S.W. Corner

(j) Move Pine Compost to new heap

3 or 4 Wheel Barrows

a cracked ashtray, house reject, full of Luckies smoked down to the roach, and a warty black rubber gardening glove.

Cornelia selects two pairs of clippers, one short, one long-handled—a giant's scissors—the kneeling mat, and a bushel basket, and returns to the garden. With the hand-size shears she attacks a hollow black cane. An aphid runs across her thumbnail, and as she pulls away the cutting, blood seeps from a scratch on the back of her left hand. The bush looks about the same as before.

(Imagine, though, how handsome they will all look in June, the rose time. Full, shapely, crowded with roses, flaunting their wealth, asking to be robbed. Helen Traubel. Queen Elizabeth.)

The bushel basket fills all too quickly; Cornelia fetches a plastic garbage pail, which is also in the garage. She dumps an armful of immense pretzel-stick cuttings into the pail. Ouch. A thorn jabs smartly right under the cuticle; red spot blossoms like a rose around it.

It will take several days for the black thorn to work its way out; part of it will grow right along with Cornelia, a bump in the fingernail, until it reaches the tip of her finger and she pares it off, three months later.

Her mother's call: "Cornelia, come in out of the *rain!*" Hack, cut, pull. Bleed. The drizzle increases to downpour, trickling off the branches, down her nose, smearing to black when she tries to wipe the rain from her eyes, puddling in the bottom of the cutting pail.

She drapes a piece of burlap over the cuttings and squashes the whole thing down with a sneakered foot. Surveying the damage. Eight clothes poles at the edge of a thicket. The rain falls faster. The amateur works harder, demolishing another, another—snip—she has accidentally severed all three canes of a live John F. Kennedy.

Come out of the rain, Cornelia, you can't possibly finish them now. Dump the wet wood on the compost heap (where the gardener does not wish for it to be; the thorns will be wounding him all summer), put away the tools. The shears are rusting fast. Wipe your face and go inside.

* * * * *

"Pea, Dwarf, Tall. GROWING SUGGESTION: Plant as early as ground can be worked."

* * * * *

"It's no use, Mother. I can't get the roses done. I can't even *think* about the vegetable garden. Couldn't we hire somebody?"

"He'd hate that, somebody he doesn't know, doing it wrong. Stealing his fun."

"Myron could at least spade up the soil, couldn't he?"

"Myron's promised to the Sanderses this Saturday. He'll be out the weekend after that. Anyway," the mother says, "I *have* tried. In the Yellow Pages. Madison Square Gardens and Collangelo. They were solidly booked. Why, you're soaking wet!"

* * * * *

There comes a sound of rivalry by day: Sissy with the children. "Hi, Nana! Hi, Poppa!" shouts the two-year-old, who's been practicing that greeting in the car all the way from New York City. "Hi, Poppa!" He races through the swinging doors into the living room.

"Poppa's not here, Kenny," says his grandmother.

"Hi. Poppa?" He shoots out his lower lip, bursts into tears.

"Kenny threw up in the car. (Hi, Cor.) I can only stay a second. I was Visiting. He was eating Jell-O. Cornelia, are you pruning the roses? He says to get the tomatoes in and if possible the peppers, never mind the onions. He'll do them when he gets home. He drew me a diagram. (Where is it?) They should be about a foot deep and six inches apart. Oh God, maybe he said six inches deep and a foot apart. Chuck, the freezer is empty. (He just had a Good Humor.) But it's raining," says the younger sister, suddenly dejected.

"And the soil hasn't even been turned," Cornelia says.

"All right," their mother tells them, over an armful of Kenny and Chuck, "I'll call Collangelo's again."

* * * * *

Phone call: "The strangest thing happened this morning. I was looking out the window when I saw a little yellow pickup truck coming right up the driveway. Two men got out. One of them went around the front of the house and the other into the garage. Then they both came back, got into the truck, circled the turnaround, and drove straight off without ringing the doorbell or anything. I think they were the men I hired to cut the grass and see about the gardens. Maybe they'll come back when it stops raining?"

* * * * *

"Good morning, madam. Mr. Tredeci. You got something for me to do with a garden?" A husky man with a soft accent is standing at the kitchen door.

"Are you Madison Square Gardens?"

"No, ma'am. Tredeci."

"Well, Mr. Tredeci, you've come at a bad time. It's my husband who should be giving you the instructions. I'm afraid during the last month he let things slide, rather. Tredeci? That's funny, I don't remember calling you. However, since you're here. I'll show you where it all is," says the mistress of the house. She takes him out to the rose and the vegetable gardens, and shows him the garage tool collection.

Whistling an Italian aria, the gardener hefts the shears.

But later, when she returns from visiting the hospital, he's gone as mysteriously as he came. And so are the electric hedge clipper, the self-charging flashlight, and the new pruning shears. The vegetable garden's unturned, the roses half pruned—their roots, however, deep in a snow of fertilizer that the gardener had intended for vegetables. A service for which they will never be billed.

* * * * *

"Did you get my tomatoes in, the Fantastics?" he asks from his hospital bed. Red globes, as bright on the inside as out, almost seedless, sweet to bite into, sweeter than raspberry Jell-O. Wilting in the garage, desperately etiolated, wanting outdoors.

* * * * *

"When seedlings have one or two pairs of leaves or begin to crowd each other, it's time to transplant."

* * * * *

Now here's Sissy on her knees, trying to tend the little boys and turn topsoil simultaneously. Pioneer woman, clearing the wilderness, 30 × 40 feet, of its winter harvest of stone, digs at it with a trowel, scrapes with the fork, tugs at an entrenched dandelion root. The dandelion, the ubiquitous plantain have spread through the lawn, encouraged by yet more rain. Today, for once, the sun is out.

The sun is baking the soil to crust, mud pie. It is painting a red streak down the nose of this other amateur.

The children are making mud pies in the cold frame, where the only growing things are the lilac clubs of wild leeks. Correction: they *were*. Actually, Chuck is making a kind of stone pie, a cairn of rock. Assisting his brother, Kenny accidentally hits him on the head.

City woman, pioneer, having soothed her brats, returns to her task, rendering dirt. Scratch, cug, like the birds. Tomato-breasted robins hunt for worms by the compost heap, where hundreds ooze and thrust in the darkness, under the rose cuttings; some of them as big as snakes. Under the birdbath, which Cornelia has filled, a blue jay and a squirrel have started a fight. Squirrel loses. Jay gives a final cheer and flies off, leaving behind a blue feather to commemorate the victory.

"Kenny, don't take your shoes off. There are sharp things in the grass."

A boy a head taller than Chuck is watching, silently, by the compost pile, as the three of them work. "Do you want to play?" Sissy asks after five minutes. "They're Mr. Holcomb's grandchildren."

Disclosing a space in the mouth which shows he's earned a dollar or two from the Tooth Fairy, he beams. "Oh, Mr. Holcomb. He's my *friend.*"

Chuck nonchalantly steps backward and sits down on some thorn cuttings his aunt failed to put into the pail.

* * * * *

"Why, Myron! We didn't expect you till next week." A dark man who claims to be complected of Africa, Cherokee, and Connecticut arrives with the rain.

"Mr. Holcomb and I, we didn't get time to fix up that garden, and I know the lawn needs doing. Anyway, I thought I'd look in on you folks. I know you want everything nice when he comes back. I promised him I'd look after you and all."

And all. Gently, she says, "There are a thousand and one jobs that need to be done. The girls have been working like demons down there. I'm afraid to look. But you can't work outside in the *rain*. You'll catch your death."

"Mr. Sanders said I could switch weekends. When it stops raining I'll do the grass. Then maybe about that vegetable garden."

"Well, if you promise to stay inside."

"Cross my heart." Weeping water, he goes down to the basement. There is work to be done in the cellar, too; they were whitewashing the walls together when the old man heard that his hospital bed was waiting for him.

There is no change in the weather, and presently, working alone in the waterproof basement, he sighs, takes an old rubber coat that hangs from a peg by the cellar steps, stiff as though there were a man inside, finds some boots and a rain hat, goes out to tend the plantation.

She catches sight of him from time to time, from an upstairs window: an old hat and a coat moving around the gardens. "Oh Ben—Myron! Come in and eat something," she calls.

He's dug up most of the goddam vegetable patch, turned it over, dragged the rake round it to curry the pebbles from the mud, but Mr. Holcomb likes it to be composted, too. Lunchless, emptying barrowfuls of compost, pushing aside the thorn-cutting topping of the mulch pile (getting only a little scratched). Next time, he can get rid of them where they belong. Rain makes soup of the rich brown mixture trickling in dilute down the slope of the lawn.

Time for him to catch his train now. But the work of turning the soil is finished. The roses are pruned. Too bad about them tomatoes. Maybe the girls can get them in. When the sun comes out and they can rake it over, making the surface fine and soft and crumbly, put in those seedlings and seeds and bulbs like he keeps asking.

Myron changes clothes again, putting the coat and hat and boots where he found them. One of the cellar doors opens to a secret staircase, a hiding hole under the porch. Slave people used to live there while they were running away, Mr. Holcomb says. Then he writes with some effort on the space at the end of a highly complicated list: "You get out of there and come home."

* * * * *

"Preparing for Outside Planting (Hardening Off): About a week before putting the seedlings in the garden, toughen them by gradually exposing them to more air and a lower temperature. . . . If you have a cold frame, use that. . . . An express wagon or cart is handy for holding flats or pots of seedlings. Wheel them out into the sun in the daytime, back into the garage or shed at night."

* * * * *

A fair day (for once) in the garden, where Sissy and Cornelia are laboring like field hands; their work is cut out for them. Sunday, busy day in the village. Automobiles converging on the three churches. Close by, a carillon plays hymn tunes. O God, Our Help in Ages Past. How Firm a Foundation.

* * * * *

"An hour or more before you transplant into your garden, water the flats or containers well, preferably with a solution of Transplantone, and let them drain. This will reduce the possibility of wilt and shock."

* * * * *

The seedlings are limp from their time in the garage, but with luck and water and plenty of sunshine they'll grow and bear tomatoes. (Not so lucky the peppers, which have already perished and gone to the mulch pile.) "Cornelia, I'll dig the holes," Sissy says. "You follow with the tomato plants."

"Yes, and they have to be watered. Where's the nozzle?"

Cornelia goes into the garage and comes out with Kenny and the brass nozzle. "He was eating an onion bulb. Now. Chuck, do you know how to turn the water on?" He does, and Kenny, who was looking up the end of the nozzle, gets an eyeful.

"Cornelia, whatever happened to those new pruning shears?"

Down by the water, sailing people are getting their boats in shape, landlubbers stroll in the park, cruise slowly by the water's rim in their cars on their way home from church. After three warm rainy days, a considerably greener town; the leaves are bigger than squirrels' ears; well past the time when the Indians said to plant corn. Pink-white blossoms on the apple trees. The children's grandmother comes out and inspects their progress; two tomato plants set in. "It's past noon: they just rang for Communion at St. John's, girls. Sissy, are you ready? It's mean to keep him waiting; let's get going."

"I have to take the children to the Noonans'." They follow their mother grudgingly—Kenny with his big lip, Chuck pretending not to care, abandoning the garden temporarily, the tomato plants dying slowly under the sun.

* * * * *

Mrs. Noonan's kitchen: "Don't cry, Kenny. Chuck, listen, I hear the Good Humor-truck bells. I'll tell you boys a story. Once upon a time there was a family of birds who lived in a hayfield and went by the name of White.

All summer long they were happy as larks, with plenty to eat and no one to pester them in the tall, warm hay. Every morning the chicks practiced flying, and every evening you could hear the mother bird calling them all home to the nest: 'White! White! White!' Then one afternoon Momma White went scurrying to find her husband. 'Bob White! Bob White! The most terrible thing! I heard the farmer talking to the hired man. He said, "Sam, the hay's getting pretty high in the South Forty. Better get out your mower and cut it tomorrow." He'll cut down our nest and our chickens can't fly yet. Bob White, what are we going to do?' 'Not to worry, Momma,' says Bob. 'Our chicks will be ready to fly any day now.' 'But tomorrow the mowing man's coming, with his terrible long, sharp blades.' 'The farmer's gone to town to sell some pigs. They'll have their wings before the mower comes.' Next day the hired man went out to cut the hay, going round and round the field with his mowing machine. The little Whites heard the blades and were frightened, but Bob White told them, 'He won't come near our nest today.' Sure enough, the sun got hot and the hired man decided to take a nap under the big shade trees. When he woke up it was sundown, so he called it a day and went home. Next day: 'Bob White! Bob White! I hear the hired man cutting down the hay. My chickens can't fly yet. What, what shall we do?' 'The farmer's still away, my sweet,' says Mr. White. 'The hired man won't do the job today.' The same thing happens. The hired man cuts down a little bit more of the field. And the next day, too. But that night Mr. White hears the farmer driving up, back from the town. 'Well, Sam, how did you make out with the South Forty?' and the hired man replies, 'I've had a bad piece of luck with the mower. One horse got a stone in its hoof.' 'Hmm. Well,' says the farmer, 'I guess I'd better do it myself.' Bob White scurried home. 'Momma White! Are the children ready to fly?' 'I think so, Bob.' 'The hay will be cut tomorrow for sure. Get set to fly!' Bright and early next morning the farmer hitched up his horses and went out and cut down the hayfield. Just as the blades reached the nest, the little birds rose out of the hay, whir, whir, whir, whir, whir and up into the sky, safe from the mower with its long, sharp blades. 'You see,' said Bob as they all went soaring. 'What the farmer tells the hired man to do is one thing, but when the farmer says he'll do it himself, it gets done.'"

* * * * *

The women of the house are back from the hospital. Sissy goes next door to collect her children, Cornelia and her mother to the garden. There they find a large-hatted lady kneeling by the tomatoes; tomato plants, seven of them, march down a row, beginning to lift their leaves like wings.

"Whew, I think I'm getting sunstroke," Alice says. "I just dropped by to see how things are and noticed Ben's tomatoes not getting any healthier. Once you get started, it's hard to stop," she apologizes, red-faced middle-aged lady planting somebody else's tomatoes.

"Who's that?" Cornelia asks. A white Chevrolet grinds up the driveway, and the Forsters step out, still in church clothes.

"Nobody answered, so we just decided to drop these on the doorstep." Polly Forster has packages under her arm, a crossword-puzzle book for the mother. "And I thought he'd like to see the new Agatha Christie."

"Who pruned Ben's rosebushes?" Robert Forster asks. "Not a bad job. You should chase those aphids, though. Mine were crawling with them. And your Peaces need to be cut back some more, they're too leggy. Let me show you."

He fetches shears from the garage, begins to clip. "I poked around for those new rustproof, spring-action, super-sharp, carborundum-coated shears I saw him buying uptown the other Saturday, but they've vanished. Say, you ought to do something with those onions in the garage, they've sprouted."

"Where do you think they should go?" Cornelia asks.

Her sister, Kenny, Chuck, and a neighbor child joining them, along with Mrs. Noonan, who is, as always, pregnant. "How too bad about Mr. Holcomb. We haven't known each other very well, but Georgie and Billy are over here all the time, helping him out. I think Mr. H. let them bury a dead bird. We all love to see the gardens—Jim and I certainly intend to ask his advice about getting one in ourselves. Whenever we stop having babies. Can I help?"

"We better go, Robert."

"Oh, stay awhile," begs the gardener's wife.

But Robert and Polly are back half an hour later, having changed to gardening clothes, with their son Ronald, whose number in the draft lottery came up unlucky and who is fighting to become a conscientious objector. "I helped with plenty of jobs for your father last summer," he informs Cornelia. "Boy, can he work!" He shakes his head, starting on the onions. "He always made me take home stuff for the salad. I used to think dill was just a brand name for pickles."

Another car enters the by now crowded driveway turnaround; it's the Sanderses, the sharers of Myron, who live in a house as old as this one. "We heard you were having a garden party, so we brought you some bell-pepper plants. Stan got greedy at the seed store."

The doctor next door, whose wife has been nagging him to clip the hedge that partitions their properties, looks down from the stepladder, sees the party, and joins them.

Mrs. Noonan comes over again, with a couple more children and some homemade brownies, the recipe for which is sought by the women (Betty Crocker). Sissy, eagerly assisted by her sons, finds ice cream and cold drinks and brings out more refreshments. Cornelia lugs the rickety table from the garage to the grass to put them on. And packets of seeds: beets, carrots, pumpkins, Bibb lettuce, Oak Leaf lettuce, chicory, romaine, sage, parsley, zucchini, peas, green beans, radishes, sweet corn.

Corn?

(His intention was to start a new garden for corn and the late-bloomers, squash, pumpkins, and gourds; never mind.)

Well, maybe one short row of corn.

* * * * *

"The professional way to go about garden planning is to lay it out to scale using a sheet of graph paper."

Bob Forster, a professional art director (whom Myron will spot at the Red Radish in Greenwich Village next Thursday night escorting a woman younger than Polly), reads off the directions on the backs of the seed packages, writes idly along the back of an envelope:

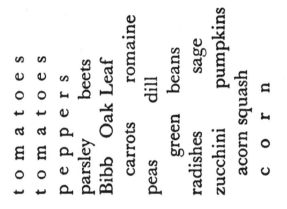

and, laid out first on paper, then under their hands, a garden takes shape. "Joe, where the hell are you?" a woman next door is calling. Finishing her tomato job, Alice, whose Jack slipped on their yacht, struck his head on the dinghy, and drowned one summer, begins on the peppers. The son of the Sanderses, who once planted a chestnut by the house (the tree is tall as the roof now), would surely be here, were he not serving an eight-month term in the state reformatory for pushing marijuana at the local high school.

But the people in the garden have other matters to discuss: horticulture, the absent gardener.

"These bulbs look like something's been eating them."

"The raccoons have been out of hand this year."

"Look, there's *more* of that *Cyperus* he divided and gave me a clump of. I've gotten three plants out of it already. I almost wish they would stop spreading."

"I see he's building another compost heap. He made me stick my arm in it up to the elbow once, so I could see how hot it was inside."

"Kenny, darling, you're standing right on the cucumbers. Oh, you're helping Mommy plant, too. Well, those are petunia seeds, baby. I guess they'll look real pretty with the cucumbers. . . . Goodness, I thought they were cucumbers. I guess the petunias will look real pretty with the Swiss chard."

"Mona, Stan," the gardener's wife remembers. "That time during the war when hoodlums destroyed the Yokonabes' Victory Garden! (You went to kindergarten with Toby Yokonabe, Cornelia.)

"And the next day everybody came over and replanted it for them. Strangers, neighbors." (The Yokonabes, who were denied membership at any of the beach clubs, moved away as soon as the war was over.)

"Polly, are you sure you've got the right end of the onions up?"

* * * * *

By five o'clock the garden is weeded, seeded, watered, and ready to grow. Rows of tomato plants, row of peppers, a colorful random growth of seed envelopes inverted on ice-cream sticks from Billy Noonan's collection—*all* the seeds, including those the gardener meant to reserve for succession plantings—signs expounding the harvest to come, billboards for starlings (and, for carrots, a tombstone). Polly has planted the onions upside down, and some of them were hyacinths, but it doesn't matter; there will be onions. Next spring a solitary purple hyacinth will erupt from the bare earth in their row. Squash blossoms may never pollinate and set, raccoons may eat the lettuce, corn mildew, there will be too many gourds, who cares?

Amiable, smug, kind and bigoted, unfaithful, loyal, mortal, they all stand back and admire the job they've done.

* * * * *

Two weeks later, the neat brown area is filmy with seedlings, some of them uninvited, not all as represented on the seed packets. The convalescent, home from the hospital at last, can't wait to get a look at his property. He goes slowly around the house, checking all: lawn ragged, tulips need separating, beech branch fallen almost in the driveway. Making a mental list, (1) Hospital azaleas by the flagstone path to the veranda. (2) Clip hedge.

They show him his rose garden, his vegetable garden. The high-shouldered tomato plants too close to the soil's top, the puny peppers, the salad vegetables, herbs, beets he might never have thought to see; he blesses them, weeds and all. "Wonderful! You've done a great job! Couldn't have done it better myself." And the black squirrel scampers up the elm tree.

Passengers

A FATHER AND HIS CHILD ONE DAY set out to see the world. Or anyway, to see what they could see. Just a small piece of it, really, where there's a thing an old friend told him about he's always intended to take a gander at, a natural feature of the landscape, a cliff, canyon, or ravine, carved back then by the glacier, with a trail they could walk down, single file like Indians—a gully, an arroyo, a gulp—

Imagine that, a Gulp!

His wife, who couldn't find him in the kitchen, has sent her daughter out to the terrace, where he is discovered beaming over a cup of coffee, his gardens full of early fall flowers, zinnias, yellow and gold, the world in general. "Did you ever see a grander day?" It's the temperature of early summer, windless, the sky flawless through the shade trees, like looking up through a blue balloon. Only a telltale cicada announces the real time of year, with a raspberry from the silver maple in the center of the lawn.

He explains, "Well, a gap, or a gulf. Here it is! The Gorge!" He's got out a couple of map books and is leafing through the Hagstrom *Atlas to Fairfield County.* Mort Martin told me about it and I marked the place. When I woke this morning it dawned on me—let's go! We can paint the terrace some other time."

"Why, Ben," says his wife, coming out to see where everybody's gone. "I thought you were going to take it easy today. Anyway, the weather report says rain."

"Well, I've certainly never been to a Gulp," the daughter says. "Maybe Mother could lend me some sneakers?"

"You go ahead, then," says the older woman with resignation. "I'll make you some sandwiches. I'd come too, but I think I'm getting a cold."

"You think everyone's getting a cold, Mother."

They go into the garage and get into the car, a powerful green Oldsmobile without much mileage on it, and he backs out, expertly clearing the two inches on either side of the garage doors, and shoots off down the driveway just in time to miss the woman coming out of the kitchen door with a sweater for her daughter.

Since the Sound is nearby, they drive down for a look—a blue untarnished mirror, vacant, today, of sailboats, and, around by the beach, nearly deserted. Then up the main avenue of the village peninsula, under beeches and maples, past big houses with big neat lawns, where blackbirds and flickers are beginning to gather to migrate, though the leaves retain their chlorophyll. Blue jays come crashing in like 747s.

A jet flies overhead. "Rackety things. Our congressman promised to reroute them," he says, "but no one seems to have informed the pilots." They're passing the town library, across from the firehouse, right before the Post Road.

"Better under one than on one," says the passenger, lifting her voice.

"And are you still afraid to fly?" The delayed sound effect, catching up, drowns out her response.

Crossing over the railway tracks and the Thruway, they leave the town and head west toward the Parkway. The two-lane road is busy, like the air, as though everybody in Westchester had somewhere important to go today.

"May I drive?" she asks, with real yearning.

"Later, when we hit the back roads. It would make me nervous."

"Well, who taught me to drive?"

As they reach the crowded Parkway, he hesitates, doesn't turn. "Let's try a new way. Let's just meander."

As he reminds her, Meander is not a Greek playwright but a river in Turkey which wanders in coils, and hence a name for any wayward river or stream—for example, a brook in a cow pasture. The water, flowing downward, will always curve back and forth, like the lash of a whip, with gravity for the handle. Snaking back and forth, until the coils merge and form a lake or marsh and time dries them up, or digging downward and etching the surface beneath into a canyon, straight walls through which it can travel in a straight line, true, trapped forever, until the next ice age. (This Gulp or Gorge will probably illustrate the effect.) Scientists, like cows, are familiar with the phenomenon but, he read in *Scientific American*, haven't come to any conclusions.

"Give them a chance. They haven't had as long as the cows."

And so they meander in a northerly course, through small settlements full of traffic lights, past country clubs with close-cropped golf greens, into opener country. Three polled Herefords in a field, staring at the airplanes. "Oh," he sings, "Cows and cattle/ Grazing there/ Among them all—"

"—The Old Gray Mare!" A silly song composed for children when as a family they went for Sunday drives.

She studies the atlas—pages of all-too-detailed maps with too many street names, and enigmatic clues ("For adjoining area see map no. 10, page 31"), like a Parker Brothers' board game.

"Pop, what state is this Gulf in, anyway?"

He can't recall, but it should be near the border. A river, end product of meander, like the Grand Canyon.

On page 31, the directive's penciled in: *See Atlas for Fairfield County.* The odometer hits the twenty-five-thousand-mile mark. A tangle of green foliage rising on each side of them, coarse second- or third-growth woods, they ride through an amorphous, tree-crowded landscape, with bends the driver can't see around. Here and there a branch of swamp maple, prematurely turned, shows the red feather. They are apparently in a section of Westchester or Fairfield County that has not yet been mapped or explored. She tells him they're lost. He accepts the news approvingly. "Terra Incognito! Fine!"

But up there in the sky a glider circles, probably not far from an airfield, the hot sun at meridian casts compass needles of shadows. To the east, the hum of cars on the Parkway. You can't be truly lost in Westchester County. (Or Fairfield?)

Ascending a steeper hill, a true back road, perhaps one of the last in these parts to have been tarred. "Stop," the driver tells himself, and brakes. "What does that sign say?" A wooden arrow points into the woods: "Appalachian Trail."

"It can't be. The Trail doesn't come this way. I walked every inch from Connecticut to Canada once, the autumn after I first came East. With a backpack and an ax. What I really wanted was to walk the whole way in the springtime from North Carolina—following the spring north. Oh well," he reflects, "life is a series of major and minor disappointments." (He has said this many times.) "But let's just see where it goes. Stretch our legs. Bring the sandwiches, I'm hungry as a horse."

* * * * *

A very short way up, the trail opens onto a field, near the top of the hill, yellow with goldenrod pungent under the strong sun. At the woods' edge, they blink. The power lines run at an angle through the field, in the avenue that has been cleared for them; the poles with the lines strung between them march straight as a furrow down the hill and up another, regular as the rest bars on a music staff. He smiles. "I always thought I'd like the job of lineman—walking the Electricity Trail. I'll bet you could follow the power lines all across the country."

She peers out. "I think I see the Sound." A hard, very distant glitter of light to the east. (Or could it be the Gulp—the cut, the rivery wildland, the narrow gorge, the white water with the hemlock needles perpetually falling?) They sit on a stone wall to consider the view, unwrapping and eating the sandwiches the one who stayed at home has prepared—tunafish-and-lettuce on rye, with the crusts neatly trimmed off. The cicadas here, too, buzzing from a pole.

The power lines remind him of a ski tow. "Will you ever forget the one in Vermont? When we collected you after camp and you were afraid to ride up the mountain?"

Yes, she remembers. The high wires of the ski tow, operating in the summer for tourists, flimsy chairs dangling overhead, specks disappearing over the horizon. He persuaded her to get on, explaining about the tensile strength of the wires. "Why, an elephant could ride safely on one of these things." Chuckling over the picture of an elephant on skis, they got on. "It was fun! A beautiful ride," she says. Fear dropping away with the grassy slope, the riders soaring over the treetops, into the sky, toward the summit.

"*You* loved it. I was scared to death."

"Well, I wanted to walk down, too."

The power lines hum, and the insects, seeking the end-of-summer flowers—goldenrod, purple aster, blue thistle. Many fall flowers are blue, he says, because the short rays of the spectrum are best seen by insects in the sun's longer rays. Indeed—

They each spot a patch of blue flower heads, near the place where they entered the field—the closed gentian, nearly invisible until you have seen it, and then indelible, blueness itself, *Gentiana andrewsii*, thriving in the darkness on the brink of October. They go over to look closer. She reaches down to pick one but he stays her hand, no. They're rare, an endangered species. Nevertheless, he wistfully imagines them into one of his gardens. "I wonder if they'd grow. By the rhododendrons. Near the terrace."

Which gives him a real idea. "I've been meaning to start a wild garden." He moves toward the light, where among the goldenrod and asters stand relicts of August, gone to seed and pod—yarrow, tansy, Queen Anne's lace, and thistle. The wayside, alien flowers which follow the path of European man, imported with him over the sea.

They harvest the old flower heads at random. Boneset, Saint-John's-wort, common everlasting, pussytoes. He named them all for her once. "I used to think you made those names up," she tells him now. Milkweed feathers stick to his shirt, and seeds leak into her borrowed sneakers. "Do you really think they'll grow?" she asks.

"No doubt about it," he says with authority. "Weeds always do." They will, for sure, spring up and likely spread to the lawn, to join the dandelion and the ubiquitous plantain. The work of a gardener (and his handyman) is never done.

"Well, I guess that's enough," he says, reluctantly. They stuff flower heads into the paper bag that had held their lunch, leaving out a half-eaten sandwich for the porcupines or raccoons, and she carries the overflow. "I would like to get home and plant these now," he says. "We can look for the Gulp another day. Do you mind?"

"Not at all."

He looks around once more. Woods, field, sky, water, electric lines. *"Et in Arcadia ego."* (Pronouncing it "eego.") " 'I too have been in Arcadia,' right?"

She hesitates. "Approximately."

And so they throw the dry things in the back seat and start back the way they came, and rather soon the Parkway crosses beneath the road, and they're in familiar territory again, Terra Cognita. They plunge right into Parkway traffic, no longer meandering. A Heraclitean river, with every car a different make of molecule, Chevrolet, Pontiac, Cadillac, Oldsmobile, Volvo. Work to do at home now—a new chore. He hunches over the wheel as if the car (he didn't let her drive) were trying to get away from him.

"Try and remember everything you've passed, and when you go back—make the first thing the last."

Off the Parkway, back over the Thruway and the railroad tracks, and the shopping section near the station, the ice-cream store, and a memory strikes her. "Pop, remember when you used to drive us around the village with our eyes closed?"

"Shut-eye night ride!" A Pop who never outgrew baby talk.

In the back seat, the little girls shut their eyes, with the aftertaste of ice-cream sundaes in their mouths, and in the darkness try to read a mental street map while the driver outfoxes them, making unexpected turns, tangling the route, taking them home every time a different way. The car goes straight where they imagine it should curve; it seems they're being driven at twenty-five miles an hour into a wall, a picket fence, a hedge—the children cringe, anticipating the crunch of metal on stone, or leafy wood wrapping itself around the car, precursor of this one (1941 Studebaker. Later he taught them to drive it).

The car with its passengers (in this dream ride) dashes out onto the Post Road without waiting for the light, dives right through the side of the A&P and out, soundlessly, through the picture windows of their friends' living rooms, plunges into the waters of Long Island Sound. "Now." Drawing grandly to a stop. "Where are we?"

"Willow Avenue," "Second Village," the daughters guess.

"Open your eyes." A strange house in a cul-de-sac—suddenly familiar. "The *Sanderses!*" Or, a perfectly new street they've never been on before, on the far side of town. Or—more often than not—by the water, the lights from Long Island twinkling. Always, they open their eyes reluctantly; guessing where you are isn't as much fun as guessing where you were, and besides, the journey is over, the ice cream is gone, bedtime. They never really wanted the ride to be over.

* * * * *

They make the customary tour of the water's edge in the green Oldsmobile, all eyes open. The weather forecasters may have had a point. The blue gone out of the sky and the water, dark as ice tea, agitated. Neap tide or a distant sea storm. The beach is littered with sweet-gum balls, tracked with footprints like an unmade bed; the bathers have emptied the bathhouses and a family is dragging a small boat out of the water. Up the driveway and "Home again on the same day!" says the driver, as usual.

He rests in the car for about thirty seconds, and she removes their harvest from the back seat.

"Let's get these things in before it rains."

He selects a site near the doctor's house next door, half rock, half crabgrass, under a dwarfed and aging willow. With rakes they scrape away the grass roots. "I've always wanted a wild garden," he repeats, the husbandman, custodian of the tame—a place for the weeds he has to kill everywhere else to live. Maybe the rabbit, mole, and starling will feast from there and leave his roses, vegetables, and zinnias alone. A miniature rocky field for tiny cows—he will imagine them grazing there at the edge of the pasture, heads bobbing, the scent of dry earth-flowers, spicy: tansy, yarrow, Queen Anne's lace. Perhaps the thistle-loving goldfinches will come to the thistles when it's their time to roam between summer and fall. And, hey, what it really needs is a place for the cows to plash, making hoofprint puddles: a stream, a meander—a fountain? An elaborate construct of pipes. Absently he hums the sad tune "Cows and Cattle":

She helps him break up the flowers and scatter the seeds on the surface of the raked place. He begins to tell her about the fountain-meander but she doesn't attend, staring at the sky, where a flock of blackbirds crisscross over the silver maple, making up their collective mind about when to go south.

"Do you know," he says, looking at them too, "I saw the last passenger-pigeon flocks in Iowa. Not like in the old days when there were billions, but enough to literally darken the sky. When I was a kid, of course. And a few years later they stopped coming down the Mississippi." He inspects the dirt and flowers.

She asks, "Do they need compost?"

"No, water. Plenty of water."

The two of them unravel the heavy coils of the hose and sprinkle the rock-garden meadow with water that trickles down the slope in branches and puddles (like tiny hoofprints). He's not quite ready to quit.

"Don't you want potting soil to take back to the city? I've got compost to burn!"

"What would I do with it?" she wonders. But he insists on teaching her the science of mixing potting soil, working rapidly in the latening afternoon, for warmth, panting in the chilly wind from the Atlantic. Directing this show now, he calls for wheelbarrow, spade, and a window screen (a spare). The mixture is one part homemade compost from the compost pile, rich and brown as cocoa, to two parts soil from the vegetable garden, spaded up and sieved into a bushel basket. He lets her do the dirty work—dig and sift the soil into one basket, heap compost into another, and scoop it all into the wheelbarrow with a coffee can. Two cans of soil to one of humus.

She fetches some A&P paper bags she finds under the kitchen sink. He looks for different sizes of flower pots in the potting shed annexed to the garage, and shows her how to pot: fill in around the bottom hole with terra-cotta shards of old pots, for drainage, then with the soil, almost to the top. Exactly the way he is going to plant his tulip and hyacinth bulbs soon, to bloom in February, his portable indoor winter garden.

The packages of soil and pots are as heavy as though they were filled with water. In the kitchen, they tie them with cord, and her hands tingle and burn as they set them on the back porch so she won't forget to take them on the train with her to the city. And from Grand Central to the subway, from the subway, home. The string may hurt her hands, but she'll manage. And stow them in any available corner, till she can find a use for them.

He mixes a drink for each of them, and they take their glasses outside to the cement terrace (the only green place in the yard that never has to be weeded or mowed) to savor one of the last of the outdoor evenings, before the clocks are turned back. He eyes its scabrous surface. "It needs to be painted. Come out again soon. You and your mother could help, sweeping off the leaves." He sits down. They set their drinks on the white tin table and relax in the swingy outdoor chairs he'll have to wash and put away soon, with the aid of Myron, the dark handyman. The table is starred with the outlines of leaves fallen from the trees overhead.

The sky is pale gray, the sun, near the horizon, invisibly veiled. "It does look like rain," she says.

He sighs. "We don't need it. We've had over three inches in my rain gauge this month so far."

"Peter," calls a cardinal in the hedge, and close by a chickadee ogles the bird feeder that dangles over the terrace from a maple branch.

"Otherwise, it's been a good summer, a first-rate growing season." Light ebbing ever so slowly.

"Phoebe." A flock of chickadees in the branches behind his head, like music notes. One of them snatches a seed and flies up to a branch to crack it.

"Pop, tell me some more about this gorge."

"It is supposed to be one of the last wild places around, virgin forest, an Indian burial ground. Come out again soon. Maybe I'll even let you drive."

Airplanes from Spain circling Kennedy Airport. Sweaterless, she shivers. "Jay, jay," one whoops from the feeder. The sound of cars on the Post Road, zzz of the seventeen-year locust, white noise in the white light.

"Where's Mother?"

"Upstairs. She thinks she's got a bug, the grippe or the flu."

"I'd better go up and say goodbye."

"So soon? You are always saying goodbye," he says.

"I haven't always felt welcome."

"Ah." He sips at his drink. "That was your mother. You know, I rather liked the man, in spite of everything—"

"Sow *weeds!*" Peverly, the white-throated sparrow, scratching for some fallen seeds with its feet.

"Funny. While you were away, she checked the newspaper every day to see what the temperature was there. So she could tell what you were wearing."

Indians live there in primitive splendor; they drink from the fountain of youth the Spanish tried to find, El Dorado. A place of trees and fountains and birds, Grand Canyon practically in your back yard, white water.

Loud tufted titmouse, mimics the chickadee whistle.

Feebly, the piercing, plaintive tune.

(A glen, a glen, and the fountain of youth at the center, a spring rising like a small fountain at its heart.)

She asks if he is still busy with the volunteer firemen.

"The ambulance corps is thinking of buying an ambulance," he says, proudly.

And the library committee?

"Hardly leaves me time enough to read. I got some good books, though, about your ancestors—a scrappy bunch, always tangling with the Indians. Did you know one of them modeled for a character in a book by Fenimore Cooper?"

Indians in the dark, wailing for their lost property. We have burned their fortresses, stolen and tarnished the golden font.

"Remember the time I left you at the library?"

Of course—a little girl on a cold day, shivering on the stone steps, too silly to start walking the short way home, standing and shivering for two solid hours because he'd promised to collect her, and just plain forgot. *She* would forget if he didn't keep taking the memory out, like a book.

"Will you ever forgive me?"

He'll probably be asking her that for the rest of his life, too, and she will, of course, always forgive him.

"Cigarette?"

She accepts, and watches the way he opens the book of matches and strikes a light for her, cupping his hand to shield the thin flame flickering in the twilight. "Do you know the best advice you ever gave me? 'When lighting a cigarette outdoors, always use two matches.' " He laughs and lights a cigarette for himself.

The last chickadee of the evening is coming to the feeder.

Cigarette smoke curls up from each chair like a question mark.

And from an upstairs window the woman who watched the weather looks down, and she sees the smoke and frost of his breath.

Shut Eye Night Ride

FINALLY IT IS TIME TO PUT THE TOOLS AWAY and come out of the garden for the winter. The roses rest, pruned and dormant, programmed to develop thousands of new buds next season. Lawn won't need mowing till May. Perennial garden mulched, bulbs buried in the cutting garden, brand-new compost pile under the willows beside the fence with a couple of pickets missing that separates his house from the neighbors', worms stirring in the 130-degree-Fahrenheit alembic, changing leaves and coffee grounds to nitrogen-heavy mold. The people who moved out of the house next door bequeathed him a playgroundful of equipment—slide, swings, seesaw, jungle gym—for the grandchildren. An attractive nuisance, unstable Tivoli by the side of the house, which he's got to plant deeper, in cement. (One child's already taken a slow-motion, heart-stopping backward ride—the rocking swings pulling their legs out of the rain-soft ground like an iron insect—but suffered only minor damage.)

He and Myron have put away the screens and installed the storm windows, drained the boiler and reset the thermostat on the furnace for cold months. Virtually nothing left to do outside, time for indoor activities, basement puttering: working on the boat fittings, if you have one, checking all doors and lintels against drafts, to keep in the furnace heat. Suburban people empty their beach-club lockers, take down the tennis, nets, get anti-freeze for the car, and drive home to keep warm and play bridge.

Boats in dry-dock, the gates to the beaches unlocked only or weekends, when people come down to feed the geese who take shelter in the storm-frayed sandy cove. Sand littered with sweet-gum fruits like hibernating hedgehogs. The cyclists ride slower and more cautiously on sluggish wheels, play outside briefly in the pre-equinoctial light, come in, and do their homework before dinner.

Those sojourners the winter birds—chickadees, juncos, gold and purple finches, white-throated sparrow who sings "Old Sam Peabody Peabody Peabody," house sparrows, iridescent jays, and, of course, the cardinal, bright as a maple leaf even now—appear and reappear at the bird feeders the gardener has bought or made, devouring their own weight thrice a day with the appetites of birds. He watches them through the double windows of the solarium, Roger Tory Peterson on the glass-topped table where people eat in summer. New ones come periodically. Report of evening grosbeaks from the new neighbors across the lawn, who also keep a tray for the insatiables. He's never seen an evening grosbeak, and sits hopefully in wait, though he can tell of painted buntings and skies darkened with passenger pigeons, from his childhood in Iowa.

More bulbs, thirty pots full, are in different parts of the cellar: (1) Nether Darkness, beneath the wings of the slanting cellar doors, (2) Inner Sanctum, a vestibule between the inside and outside doors, and, finally, in the coolest corner of the basement itself—so that from January on there will always be one hyacinth blooming, about to bloom, or just past. He writes the color on the pot: "Delft." "Pink." When with plenty of water and judicious inattention they are ready, he'll wrap the pots in tinted foil and take them upstairs or give them to friends, and, ivory, purple, rose, their sculptured petals will release fragrance like a spilled bottle of perfume in whatever room they're in, an artificial, top-heavy five-day wonder, spring in February and then bye-bye, bulbs specifically bred to spend all their color and sweetness in a forced hothouse blooming, and to be dumped as soon as they're rancid and the tips of the spiky leaves overgrow the flower and turn yellow and the stalks lean at a forty-five-degree angle, bent down with the creamy or violet weight, encephaloids, rank—you can't replant these hyacinths, they won't divide. By February, his forced plants will be all over the village.

Extract the translucent plastic wedge of the rain gauge his wife ordered from a catalogue, one of the best presents he ever got; stow it somewhere in the garage. It can't measure snow precipitation (ten inches of snow to one of rain), and it would freeze and crack. Wash down the garden furniture and put it away under black plastic covers. D-Con for the house attic, so the black squirrels won't take up residence, and for the garage loft, where one already has. Think once more about moving to a smaller house or Florida; we're not getting any younger. All this furniture—where did it come from?—that we don't need, the youngsters could use.

Halloween, he checks the trees around the house for loose or broken branches, and in the afternoon drives uptown to collect candy for the kids who will be knocking: miniature chocolate bars, silver kisses, chewing gum, red-hots; and a twenty-pound bag of bird chow. Bowls of candy corn spread in the pantry for the beggars, and one of pennies, for their loot bags. By evening he has called it a day. Not too many children in costume will be coming all the way up their long drive, anyway, when there are so many houses closer to the street; they can afford to miss his treats this once. The grandchildren can use up his provender.

His wife telephones the families in the immediate vicinity. "Mrs. Noonan. Mr. H. feels a little grippy. . . ."

"Oh no, nothing serious, but he doesn't want the children to catch anything. We're going to turn off the porch lights so they won't ring the bell. He didn't want Billy and Georgie to be disappointed. Tell them he was looking forward to guessing who they were."

"A ghost and Spider-Man? Oh, how cute. Well, we didn't want to be spoiling their fun." Hanging up, she taps a pencil against her teeth, working the crossword puzzle. He roams around the house, setting back all the clocks to Standard Time. Then he turns off the first-floor lights and comes slowly up the stairs.

* * * * *

Thanksgiving they celebrate: the customary, elaborate, ever more copious feed, under the dining-room chandelier. All the leaves in the dining table, spread with the heirloom linen cloth. The Sheffield candlesticks and the wedding silver. The grandchildren help set the table—big spoon, little spoon, knife, dinner fork, salad fork. Dessert fork, dessert spoon. Butter knife. The blue-and-white dinner plates, with the gold ring wearing thin, the Waterford wineglasses, and the crystal goblets.

A sunbeam from the solarium strikes the chandelier, knocking light several hundred ways, sprinkling the table and the food and the faces with rainbow-colored confetti. The children paddle their fingers in the light. He breaks into song: "The fairies are dancing, tra-la, la, la, la."

She looks to see that it's all on the table and steps on the buzzer, which is a cloisonne turtle.

Sue, the maid, goes back and forth from the kitchen. Bird on the Lowestoft platter, surrounded by peaches and parsley and crab apples. The red ring of rice with peas in the middle. Cloverleaf rolls, giblet gravy, extra oyster-and-chestnut stuffing in a bowl. He carves the turkey with verve. The plates pass from hand to hand while the maid circulates with the salad, creamed onions. Champagne pops.

"Bless us, O Lord, and these thy gifts which we are about to receive from thy bounty, through Christ our Lord. Amen." From the rest of the table: "May the Lord provide for the wants of others."

The room fills with the clink of tableware and the sound of speech and chewing, often simultaneous. The mother of the little boys cuts up their food, too busy to have tasted anything on her plate. The older grandchild is very good and the little one spills.

"Sit down, Kenny."

"Gobble-gobble."

"Please pass the gravy."

"Who's ready for more turkey?" He's almost too busy to eat, too, carving up the bird for the rest of them, scooping out the stuffing. Chuck chokes on an olive. Cornelia gets the giggles; everybody catches them. They remember when, and praise the grandchildren and each other. The mistress of the house gets a word in edgewise.

Chuck and his aunt wish on a wishbone. It breaks off even.

"What did you wish for?"

"I wished it was Christmas." Bzzz. Kenny's gone under the table: the voice of the turtle. Sue rushes in from the kitchen.

"Kenny, go play until it's time for the pie."

"Pumpkin, pumpkin, gobble, gobble."

White meat, dark meat, drumstick, anyone?

"Hey, how about a toast?" proposes the little boys' father.

"What do we have to be thankful for?" asks his mother-in-law.

The head of the table rises: "To your new home! To all of us. To us old people for getting the young here, and to the young for forgiving us!" Sits down to a burst of applause and digs into the fodder to make up for lost time, while the youngest of all, the ciphers, play at his feet. Dishes fly back into the kitchen, tablecloth stained like a flag. Pumpkin pie, mince pie, ice cream, hard sauce, cheese. He takes only one helping of each.

"First time in my life I haven't had that overstuffed feeling." They're in the living room, the children working off their gobbler on the stairs. (No stairs in New York like these for them to scamper on.) Being understuffed endows the older man with energy; he remembers the untapped Halloween candy and the funny-face masks he bought for the boys.

* * * * *

Sapped and heavy from the banquet, the other relations are glad to rest while he, playing the Halloween man, answers the doorbell and the children run back and forth on the porch, and he gives them candy over and over, till even the children are panting.

* * * * *

His old and best friend comes to visit one afternoon, Mort Martin, with his wife, formerly of this village, now of Florida. Thirty pounds lighter after recovering from yet another surgical procedure. The wives bring each other up to date while the men reminisce in the basement, relive old jam sessions. He locates a bunch of scratchy 78-r.p.m. records—Fats Waller, Earl (Fatha) Hines, Gene Krupa, Satchmo. Classics. And, of course, the big-band sounds—Dorsey, Goodman.

Mellowed by a bottle of scotch he discovers in a drawer of the work desk, they compare operations and boast of their scars. Spell each other at the old Steinway he's been almost too busy to play all summer. "Liza, Liza . . ." "Tea for Two." And the wives hear music coming up from the basement, muted, like steam in the radiator. "Chinatown My Chinatown. Where the lights are low-oo—"

Then, before dark, of course they all have to see around the place, and though it's cold he marshals them outside, and points with pride. Rose garden. Vegetable garden. Cutting garden. Perennial garden. Wild garden. Old compost heap. New compost heap (next spring he'll fence it). Newly laid flagstones along the walk entirely lined with azaleas sent to him when he was in the hospital. "Nearly broke my back getting them in."

Later he makes notes in a dog-eared paperback book called *Understanding Surgery*. Always the possibility of *that* in a man of his age. Pooh, it's practically a minor operation. Anyhow, he's interested in finding out what happened to Mort.

His old friends are probably on their way back to Florida this minute. As soon as he's feeling tip-top, he and his wife will be heading down themselves. You can't fool yourself, you're not getting any younger, and besides, down there it's a year-round growing season (we'll miss all the children; they can visit). Florida! He'll meet up with his friends the summer birds. Ponce de León. The Fountain of Youth.

Dreaming of Florida, he falls asleep with only minor discomfort. In the middle of the night, his wife wakes: he's awake and prowling again.

Monday he's got a cold. "Let's have a look at you in the hospital," says his friend the doctor. Tuesday, there's a shadow of doubt about the liver scan. Wednesday: False Alarm!

His wife telephones her children. "Ben's coming home!"

Thursday he vomits a stream of black bile clear across the room, a gusher. Friday he comes upon the word "obstruction" in the surgery book. Saturday he urgently suggests a consultation with another doctor.

"I was talking to him on the phone just now," his wife tells one of her daughters a little later, still holding the quiet receiver in her right hand. "He said, 'Well, I have to hang up now, they're taking me to the operating room.'"

* * * * *

It is the brightest day of winter, near the solstice, high noon and the sun half-mast, crystal clear through the bare trees. Geese on the beach coming to the hand, elegant as Englishmen at Ascot. Scared and hungry and angry, snatching stale bread crusts with beaks that could break a finger. A man who looks like him from the back is tossing crusts from a safe distance. Good day for experimental picture-taking, with the new Christmas camera purchased for oneself in advance. Steady the heavy telephoto lens with one hand and press it against the cheek as the book illustrates, swivel the geese into focus, get the range, click. Open the shutter wide, check the light meter, forgetting everything else, snap. Stop down, for greater depth of field, try to eliminate jiggle.

The camera can't record it all—the whisper of waves at the edge of the seaweed, footsteps crunching on the sand and the gum balls, the salt smell, the chill of the camera body and the firm tug of the iron beak, the goosey chatter. But as the eye cannot, as words cannot, it can catch and hold on to the fastest thing in the world, light, and show exactly the way a goose feeds, forever. Provided you have loaded it correctly. The third, mindless eye, recording a moment of extra time, when it was crystal clear and the old dead leaves made a gentle noise on their trees, and the birds came with shame to the hand. Before the man who looked like him turned away from the water.

* * * * *

"Fooled you," said Soul. "We'll see," says Body.

* * * * *

He's having the time of his life: plenty of Demerol so it doesn't hurt like before, nurses at his beck and call. Adhesions, that's the word. Always known he was an adhesive type. He feels like a billion. The temp is a little over a hundred, but that's entirely normal following this kind of surgery.

There's a sign on the door requesting *Times* and Coffee. His visitors find him cranked up in bed, writing out a Christmas list. For a man who hates presents, he has a lot of requests. Last night he knocked his glasses to the floor—they have been taped at the bridge with surgical adhesive—and this ad in the newspaper shows a thing to keep glasses in, a brass caddy, which you can buy from Hammacher Schlemmer, just what he's always wanted. And some semi-stretch heavyweight socks. And he needs another carton of cigarettes. His hair ruffled against the pillows, like a baby bird. With a tube coming out of his nose like a black worm, for the melancholy bile to flow.

"On second thought, don't bring it to me yet. Save it for when I come home."

Everyone in the room is smoking, including the nurse, and he sees them through a comfortable blue haze. Daughters perch on his bed, his wife in a chair at his side, or fussing with the flowers on the dresser.

After they've gone, he asks to be cranked down, circles the remote-control dial of the TV: nothing worth watching. Too early to ask for a shot? Vaguely worried about something, but for the life of him he can't think what.

* * * * *

"All over the abdomen," says the doctor, drunk with rage and pity. "Promise you we won't—"

"Make him suffer."

"—drag it out. Up to you, though."

"Make it as easy for him as possible."

Quickening him toward his end. Now Ben, this isn't going to hurt at all.

* * * * *

What else can you buy for a man who's already got all the good shirts he needs? Gadgets and whatchamacallits—nothing useful, things to use. Eyeglass caddy and an indoor-outdoor thermometer. *The Last Whole Earth Catalog*, a barometer, jigsaw-puzzle picture of mushrooms, Yankee bird feeder, Scott Joplin ragtime record album, and a year's subscription to *Natural History* magazine. The little boys get a cassette tape recorder, their mother a Polaroid camera. Images of their Christmas fun to bring to the hospital, a Colorpack snapshot of grandchildren and women on the living-room sofa beside the Christmas tree. (Squinting, holding it practically under his nose—the Plexiglas tube is gone, finally— "Very good shot of you all, and I see where a big piece of plaster is coming down from my ceiling."

"The first time nobody gave me any clothes! It's the best Christmas I ever had!" Pleated plastic drapes conceal the window with a view he's lost interest in, having mastered it the first day: the top of a tree he'd like to know the name of, the Korvettes shopping center, Long Island Sound, Long Island, and the cloudy sky. Not enough ambient light for black-and-white photography, even if the Reception Desk had permitted it—

"No picture-taking allowed in this hospital!"

"But it's a Christmas present."

"The Administration prohibits it. Leave cameras at the desk, please."

So the fast film can't catch the old man this time, and he sends no message on the tape recorder to the little boys, because they have already put the machine out of whack.

"Lovely, lovely. Now you better go. Take these things with you. I'll play with them when I come home." Hustling them out so he can have a shot and fall asleep again, killing time till he leaves the hospital.

* * * * *

On New Year's Day, a shining one. He spurns the wheelchair and his wife's arm, and walks out unassisted, a little weaker than after the last time but raring to go. Free at last! Greets all hospital plants in the sunroom again: more azalea, *Schefflera*, which he is told will bloom when it is five years old, African violet, begonia, red poinsettia and white, gardenia, wandering Jew. Is somewhat embarrassed by the quantity of cards and letters in his bedroom.

Cheerful—
    Don't let the doctor put one of
    those sticks in your mouth . . .
    until you know who ate the ice cream.

Artistic—
    Little pansies with eyes of blue
    Seem to look direct at you
    chirps a bluebird on a fountain by a flowering blue tree.

Pious—
    So I spend many happy hours
    In my garden of flowers
May God Bless You & Heal Your Body. Praying for you.
Gert Robbins.

Folks he hasn't heard from in years, contemporaries—
    You . . . are my favorite
    Master of Ceremonies

("A Fiat-Foot Floogey with a Floy Floy"—remember when you led
us to that in the Poconos?)

or has entertained more recently—

Dear Mr. Holcomb, I remember when you played the piano. We all sat
down and played and played and played.

Christmas always reminds me of your days as Santa. Keep up those
spirits of yours—

We had so much fun that Fourth of July—I can still hear your music
boxes.

Why are so many people writing to him now?

I still remember

writes Ronald from the University of Toronto

> going through your collection of old toys and comic books. And
> the doll house which worked. And being measured against a wall
> twice a year to see how I was growing. And swimming with you at
> the beach. And planting bell peppers in the shape of a bell.

"Do I have to answer all of these?" he asks, honestly bewildered.
"They should have saved their money."

He starts a list of all the things that wait to be done, undone by
his absence, but there are so many things *to* do; stretches out briefly,
instead, on the old green blanket and snores into his favorite cottony
pillow. Furnace trouble, the bad spot in the living room, black squirrel in
the attic? Call Bill the auto mechanic, Bill the plumber. Feed the birds.
Feed the plumber, pay the Bills. The convalescent man wipes out thirty-six debts in one afternoon and, running out of checks or money before
steam, puts stamps on fifty clean envelopes.

His wife brings up an African violet for his bedchamber, the least
furnished in the house, but he sends it back— "Makes it look like a sickroom." Nowhere to put it anyway. She sits on the green blanket. He sits
at a scratched but valuable drop-leaf table covered with stationery, books,
memos to himself, cigarette ashes, trading stamps, and coupons—the
paraphernalia required for running a house from a sickroom—on the
tippy armchair with a tear in the cushion concealed by a striped beach
towel. Besides the bed and the table and chair, the room contains a chest
of drawers, a bookcase, books (*Gardens Are for Eating*, the *Wise Garden
Encyclopedia*, Ivy Compton-Burnett, *Alec Templeton's Music Boxes*, *The
History of Jazz*, *Times Three*, *The Memorial History of Hartford County,
Connecticut* in two volumes, *Understanding Surgery*, *I Remember Amer-
ica*, *How Things Work*, *Know Your Roses*, *An Illustrated History of Doll's
Houses*, *Glimpses of Ancient Windsor*, *Instant Weather Forecasting*, nineteen
volumes of the Pelican Shakespeare, *The Story of the Great Naturalists,*

Papillon, a missal, the latest Agatha Christie), and a wobbly standing lamp he can move from the table to the bed, with a frayed extension cord which people sometimes trip over. The rug is his nightstand, resting place for library books he is currently reading, *Scientific American*, *Time*, and a plastic water pitcher he's lifted from the hospital and found most useful. There's one picture on the wall, an etching of a twilit Colonial country house in winter, with the moon rising behind it; though mirrors are in every other room, he finds the screen of the portable television set on the dresser serves adequately when he wants to see himself ("And how do you find yourself this morning, Ben?" "Oh, I just looked in the TV screen and there I was").

The rest of the dresser top is mostly taken up by his pill collection. Out in the hall is the electric percolator he got with supermarket trading stamps, after devoting one whole day to pasting them into the booklets in orderly rows. At night, they fill it up and set it on the marble-topped hall table, with cups, spoons, and paper napkins on a tray beside it, and a small jar of apricot preserves, which he apparently likes to eat directly from the jar. He keeps the milk pitcher on the outside windowsill of his room at night so the milk won't spoil. Mornings he feels best, recharged and confident. The blue jays in the pines wake him early, and he drinks his coffee standing in the hall, after he's dressed but before he shaves, waiting for the paper and the morning mail, and sometimes the doctor, to answer his questions:

Convalescence
- *(1)* Gauze pads
- *(2)* Chance of repeat adhesions
- *(3)* Expect discomfort? if so, how much?
- *(4)* Luminal doesn't work
- *(5)* Best sleep yet last night
- *(6)* Stitches itch?

Lucky it's winter, a time when you can relax and take care of details, take care of yourself, too, because you're still needed, so it's not egotism but really charitable to pace yourself as the doctor advised.

    (a) How often up stairs?
    (b) When drive
    (c) When garden?

He rests between tasks, even naps, and finds it almost pleasant, though dangerous—no, not dangerous, because I'm doing what's good for me, getting well. But horses if they lie down may never get up again.

He sends away for the Burpee's catalogue, and orders books on genealogy and family history from the library, and one called *How to Repair Your Old Organ* because the title tickles him.

As often as the doctor allows, he patrols the house, taking stock: is astounded by the junk they've acquired, and plans to inventory the cartons, the collections, the coins, music boxes, stamps, butterflies, which will interest the grandchildren now they're getting older. Always, last thing at night, he makes sure all downstairs lights are out and locks up, because even in the suburbs you want to discourage unwelcome guests. But she wakes, footsteps overhead—he's gotten up to hunt through the attic for that box with the travel folders.

And visitors do come, though the room isn't set up for them. The visiting nurse, come to check up, lingers for an hour. Or what seems like it. A sister from Iowa drops in and stays for a month. One daughter or the other always seems to be around, sitting on the foot of the bed or, if he should happen to be in it, the armchair with the striped towel.

They talk real estate, and moving, and money, which the young ones never seem to have quite enough of. When did he ever think about money? Actually, they haven't done badly. "Someday, of course, all this will be yours," pointing with a cigarette to the bare walls and bulging closets. "We never spent more than we earned, saved something every year, to invest."

But young people live differently—he can grasp intellectually the concept that going into debt to a bank is a way to save money and a help to the economy, but he's a Depression adolescent. His son-in-law, the lawyer, who helped draw up the will years ago, offers to look over the portfolio, and he likes the idea. Someone who really understands, getting a second opinion, tossing it lightly into younger hands. Wakes at night and thinks of things to show them all, and cannot rest again until he digs them out.

He takes his medicine like a good soldier, taping an increasingly elaborate schedule to the inside of a bureau drawer: for His Eyes Only. Sleeping Tablet, yellow, 2 per night, 1 mo's refill. Red pill. Blue pill. Gantrisin. Luminal. Erythromycin for a passing cold, Terpin hydrate for the smoker's cough, aspirin just for fun. Religiously he counts a rosary of pills, like the prayers of his youth—indulgences, novenas, the Angelus, the First Fridays. Established, efficacious order; their efficacy is in your belief. Though he hasn't been to Mass in years, his faith has never been more secure. He sits in his dressing gown and stares at the television without turning it on, believing and waiting—for the newspaper, for an operation, for spring, for tomorrow.

The blue jays scream in the dense evergreens that shade the window of his room where flowers do not grow, green cavern with the blinky lamp lit even at noon. The days are getting longer, though, sun through the solstice, heading for the equinox. It's been a mild winter. He tells the temperature of the day by the rhododendrons far below his window, their hangdog leaves relaxed and feeble in the warmer weather. On cold days they furl and rattle like green fingers, like icy hands. The pink pills are helping some.

One morning, to his surprise, the rhododendron leaves are tight as closed umbrellas and he can't wake up. He can't wake up, and coffee doesn't work. He roams methodically upstairs and down, hoping to shake off the condition. At noon he sits down in his chair to try and figure it out. "I think I've got the Blind Staggers," he tells whichever relative has come in to see how he's doing.

"The pills," they reassure him. "All that medication must be playing whoopee with your system."

"They enhance each other, there's a cumulative effect."

Water on the brain. "I can't wake up." Shakes his head and lifts his hands as if pushing something away. "Too many pills. Maybe you're right. Maybe if I stop taking them for a day."

Their voices bounce around like echoes in a shower stall, one that is filling up with steam. With much courage, he gets up out of his chair and walks to the bed. Whistles wonderingly, and tries to shake his head. "I hope *dying* isn't anything like this."

Then he does nap and wakes to take nourishment—hands and murmurs, soft-boiled eggs and buttered toast. The air has darkened, like the Iowa sky where a tornado is originating, like the passenger pigeons coming on 1,000,000,000 wings.

When it is actually dark out, he surfaces from his bad dream. Someone he recognizes is standing under the lamp. "Turn it on," he whispers. "Don't tell her, but I lost my lunch. Eggs, medication, and last night's dinner, and probably yesterday's lunch, too. I feel better. Much better. It's been this lodestone around my neck. The pump. I felt the pain of it in the back of my throat while I was sleeping."

"Taken your temperature?"

"Normal." Skin white and papery. A hand to the forehead.

"Oh, this has been the worst day of my life," he says as he drops off again.

They call the doctor at a cocktail party. He tells them not to worry, he'll come in tomorrow, and tomorrow doesn't remember that they called. But "What a fool I've been," says the invalid. "I've caught a little cold again, that's all. Just a touch of flu." His face is pink again, flushed with relief. "In a few days I'll be right as rain."

Turning and turning the fact of death like a pebble in the pocket of his dressing gown, worn smooth through fingering, getting acquainted with the surfaces, the weight, smooth, compact, hard.

A cold spell. Too chilly to putter in the basement, where the hyacinths are finally putting up green tips, too hot in the attic. Disposal on the fritz. All one night they're kept awake by the creaking and snapping of branches being murdered by an ice storm, wind, freezing rain, and temperature hovering at thirty-one. Loose twigs obstruct the gutter, the bathroom shower stops up again. He postpones calling the plumber, the plasterer, and, in disgraceful pajamas and two pairs of socks, dozes off over accounts of wars his ancestors fought in.

Then comes a day when he lifts the coffee cup to his lips and realizes, positively, he's going to get well. The son-in-law driving out from New York to look over the estate papers. The daughter with the grandchildren. All is in order, stocks, portfolio papers, will he searched half the night for, some ancient comic books for the little boys. At ten he has another round of coffee. By lunch he's not really hungry, can't keep his mind on his plate, listening for the car in the driveway, the phone to ring.

At three he goes to the cellar, waters the hyacinths, which could use some, and plays a few bars of Gershwin. At four o'clock he goes upstairs, and lies down, fully dressed. Nobody comes and nobody calls. I must have got the day wrong. Just as well. The trembly feeling in the back of my legs. Maybe if I go back to the hospital and rest there, shake off this cold.

At six o'clock he is ready.

* * * * *

In the eye of the storm, I rest. I am getting worse, I am getting better. What was life like? No matter. Everything taken care of, no need for the lists, nurses bring trays, the doctor pops in to answer questions at least once a day.

He walks to the end of the corridor and back, trailing the catheter tube over his arm.

Body stirs: It hurts somewhere inside, guts, lights, liver?

Needle comes when I feel like it, sometimes even when I don't. Put it off before their visit, listen hard to what they say. Hope they don't stay long. Talk to the morning nurse about her grandchildren, and the afternoon nurse about horse races, smoke, eat when they wheel in the tray, wait for visiting hours, my wife, my children on weekends, the shot, sleep. No twinges any longer.

Like a stone in the pocket, handling in the darkness. Why am I frightened?

* * * * *

He is aroused when they come, frequently now, and is grateful to the neighbors who drive his wife in their car since his broke down, eager for her news. How the house is doing without him, his hyacinths, what the neighbors and the neighbors' children are up to. He opens his daily ration of mail from home, and reads to her the amusing messages on the get-well cards that have come to the hospital, holding them near-sightedly up to his nose. His hands (with such clean fingernails) tap rhythms on the white sheets, she kisses goodbye, leaning with some difficulty over the chrome rail around the bed. Nurse Logan bustles in. Pop goes the needle.

* * * * *

"It can't be long now."

"When?"

"Finley says, a matter of days."

He's on the Critical List. Visitors may come any time.

Get to the bank, get the money out of the joint checking account, get new checks. Get the signatures, get power of attorney. Get ready to answer if he asks. What could they say?

Upon his breakfast tray, a pamphlet to say "God Loves the Sick."

Followed by the hospital priest, who wants to hear his confession. What have I to confess? "For your penance say one Hail Mary." Then gives him Communion, a treat instead of a treatise. The taste of pabulum, dead bread, though said to be living God. Do they have intravenous Communion for patients with signs on their doors, "Nothing by Mouth"?

High-spirited, keyed up by the drugs. Blood count dropping. Should he have a transfusion?

Should he die sooner or later?

"Doctor, I feel *apprehensive*." (Why am I so frightened?)

"Relax, Ben, you're just a little toxic."

His front toenails are inch-long talons that have worked through his socks. Knees, flexed under the sheet, tremble. "They should give you a pedicure," says a well-wisher.

"I asked the night temporary. And do you know what she told me? It's against the rules."

"Only for preemies," butts in the afternoon nurse, coming in with coffee and a pot of salvia.

"She asked me if I wanted tea and I didn't, so I said, 'I'm allergic.' 'Oh, shall I put that on your chart?' "

"Help! Help!" cries the woman in the bed across the hall.

One of the visitors goes out to the desk. "The woman in 559 has been calling for some time."

"Yes, the doctors were pumping her out. She's under sedation and doesn't really know."

Though he says her cries don't bother him, they shut the door anyway. One of them sucks on a cough drop, and he asks if he can have one, too. "In addition to everything *else*, I swallowed a filling and it's made a sore place on my tongue."

Friday he charms the hospital dentist into installing a temporary filling. His elder daughter arrives in a doozie of a snowstorm and tells him the hyacinths are about out and how good he looks. Very much the way he was, in fact—rosy-cheeked and bristling white hair.

"Wish I felt as well as I looked."

She is celebrating an achievement and offers him scotch out of a Tulip cup, which he pretends to sip—he hasn't smoked in two days or eaten for four. "What happened to the woman across the hall?" she asks.

"She got better."

He tells her to crank up the top of the bed so he can see her, and congratulates her on the good news. "You know, you've gone farther than anyone in your class!" Before the night nurse is due to arrive, he remembers to call the downstairs desk to get his daughter a taxi. The minute she goes he thinks of things for her to do, and to his companion of the night dictates a list

Cornelia
Hyacinths
Solarium
Train?
socks
Myron
Collaterals

before settling down to slumber.

Next morning they give him the first shot of morphine. Happily he babbles to his younger daughter. "You must have the Steinway for your new apartment. I'll give the boys lessons. They are grand children."

"You're a grandfather."

"They take after their father."

When the visitors all come again at noon they find him out of bed, sitting up in a chair, beak-nosed and looking taller. His wife sits and holds his hand while the male nurse brings in lunch on a tray. He doesn't eat it. "Yes, oh yes, thank you," he gasps, glad of her arm helping him back to bed. They sit in the room that's for waiting in.

"He's been telling me all week what a good wife I've been."

After a while they go in to kiss his cheek, warm and scratchy. He is babbling again, toasting a whole crowd of them, a veritable master of ceremonies, a *tummler.* "How nice," he says. "Thank you." It would be a shame to try and rouse him.

He doesn't recognize the dentist. The nurses that evening are shocked by the change. Suppose they had aroused him from that morphine stupor, why, he'd have looked at them and smiled "How nice" again. And they'd have kissed him again and said, "See you again, sweetie." And he'd have closed his eyes and recommenced his urgent, peaceful whispering. Perhaps he was making a list.

Under the Weather

STIFF AS A BOARD AND BARELY BREATHING, the old man couldn't greet his visitors. It began to snow just as they left the hospital. Miles away, in the city, the black man who worked for them shivered when he saw the first flakes come down.

"Don't go," said Body.

"I will," Soul said, and whizzed free as a bird up to a corner of the hospital room, where the male nurse, who was already packing, registered the rattle of his flight, the cessation of the sound of Body breathing, with clinical detachment. He looked at his watch and, closing the lid of the suitcase, went over to the bed.

The telephones were busy. The black man went out to get loaded, and nobody paid any mind when he pounded his fist again and again on the bar. God damn it! The old man!

The mailman knocked more than once. "Everyone appreciates MONEY SAVINGS at a time of personal loss. As an inducement to purchasing *now* we are offering a 20% savings on all monuments & footstones in our 3 display studios."

Soul was lonesome immediately. He didn't appreciate the stir.

They are not lost who find the light of sun and stars and God. "What's this, Mother?"

"Another damn plastic bookmark. Throw it away."

Body burned brightly in the furnace and Soul yearned, feeling ill.

"The Holy Sacrifice of the Mass will be offered." Priests and acolytes worked around the clock. "Unto Thy faithful, O Lord, life is changed, not taken away." At the request of several different people, he was enrolled in the Salesian Purgatorial Society and participated in these spiritual bene-fits: thirty-six Masses daily in perpetuity celebrated in a Roman basilica, the merits attached to the daily recital of the Rosary by schoolboys, the prayers and good works of Fathers and Brothers. "Life is CHANGED, NOT TAKEN AWAY."

Opening her mail, the relict shook her fingers, muttered "Gruesome," and dropped advertisements into the wastebasket. "If you have any of the following things to sell, CALL OR WRITE TO: Quintuple A Abbott Merchan-dise Co."

She watered all too often the pots in the solarium—hyacinths and geraniums and the last thing he planted. And he couldn't tell her how much water to give them or the name for its blue and purple horns. The garden catalogues and the circulars addressed to him she discarded without unsealing.

"PREPLANTED . . . READY TO GROW! Just add water—your EASTER AMARYLLIS must grow and bloom, or you owe us nothing!"

Over the months Soul grew thin as blotting paper, for there was nothing to nourish him.

* * * * *

He came by United Parcel in a cardboard box heavily taped and tied with cord, addressed to the family, along with a white envelope enclos-ing statement. Heavier than it looked and smaller than one would have expected—the kind of package a bomber might have carried into a plane or left under the seat of a movie house or in a phone booth, no weight-ier than a newborn baby. She held it a moment, looking around, finally carried it into the little round green room off the entrance hall, a Victorian tea parlor, seldom used, and left it temporarily on the escritoire.

"I almost wish we could keep him," she told her daughter when they opened it later, in the living room, slitting around the top with a kitchen knife. The flaps separated. They looked in: a silver canister embossed on the lid with a six-digit number.

The daughter tilted the box and it made a grating noise, like a pailful of beach sand from below the tide line, packed, from the grainy sound of it, to the rim. Leaning forward over the table, her mother said, "Let me see the urn, the ornamental urn." It slid out with that whispery sound, a fine dust around the rim. "Oh my God, a *can.*"

What had she expected? An urn—an ornamental urn, Greek or Wedgwood, or bronze, chased with fleurs-de-lis. (That's my first husband up there on the bookcase.) Cover it with contact paper, Wedgwood blue, or leftover Christmas wrap. Decant it into one of the dozens of pantry vases there were never enough places to put, though there were sufficient roses— the blue one over there, holding three good blossoms and a bud, survivors of winter and a savage rain. Make a label for it with a photograph of contents. "Put him back." Cardboard lid over silver eye, eyeless to his flowers.

* * * * *

The rains were the result of an almost-hurricane tropical storm that spent most of a week depositing a solid portion of the Atlantic on Florida, Maryland, Virginia, Washington, D.C., Pennsylvania, Connecticut, and the Southern Tier of New York State. The President looked over the damage, from an Air Force jet. The rains washed away townfuls of houses, housefuls of furniture, people. It made a mess of the suburbs, tore the boats from their moorings, and carried away the floats at the beaches. Westchester County declared a disaster area. It rained into the garage, through the loose shingles, broken gutters. It made muck of the leaves and grass on the compost heaps. A record rainfall, more than the rain gauge could have held had it been outside instead of in the garage, where he put it last winter; he'd have had a job and a half cleaning up after the storm. But, for the first time, he could have seen the rain gauge overflow, the garden meteorologist, the man who measured the rain. The widow had gone out to see the devastation for herself while it was still raining. Now the storm was over and she was sneezing.

Which was why she hadn't dressed but was sitting downstairs in a scarlet bathrobe with her older daughter (who was wearing purple). "What's today?"

"Saturday."

"I mean what's the date? Never mind, I can tell by the *Times*. Isn't this the first day of summer?"

The other mourners come in: slim younger daughter in a black dress, carrying a round black straw hat, son-in-law in dark blue, who sat formally on the edge of the wing chair and apologized for his bow tie. ("It was the only one I had that matched.")

"Never mind, dear, you look fine."

"Gee," he said, "it's a shame you can't make it. With the weather turning out so nice and all." The older daughter was opening a can of film, which she removed and twisted into the sprockets of the camera and wound into the box. "What about the Sanderses?"

"Meeting you up there."

"Mother," the older daughter asked, "didn't Myron say something about wanting to come along?"

"Not a peep. I guess he just plain forgot." The son-in-law looked at his watch. "Well, you all better get going," she said, and sneezed.

"You wouldn't change your mind?" She shook her head, reached for a Kleenex, blew her nose, gave them the book for the priest, Father Duffy, with a check in it like a bookmark, a thermos of coffee for the road, a florist's box, a lawyerlike portfolio labeled with her husband's last name and first initial, Cornelia's camera, the cardboard box, and a letter addressed to Miss Joan Addams.

The kitchen door slammed. The furnace was off for the summer, and, Myron not having brought the air-conditioners out of hibernation, the house as still as could be, the sound of the Oldsmobile tires on gravel dying away. She moved to pick up the small silver film capsule that had rolled off the coffee table.

Tires coming back up the driveway? She went to the back door, looked out at a familiar man unfamiliarly dressed in a dark suit and neck-tie who was standing in the graveled turnaround staring at the empty garage. "Myron! You've got your weekends mixed up again."

"Didn't I say I wouldn't miss saying good-by to the guy?" He wiped his face. "The Sanderses were supposed to ride me up there, but they didn't meet my train, so I guess they forgot. Thought I could go with you people. How come the car's gone?"

"Tsk. The children left just under two minutes ago. Oh, it's so dear of you to have gone to all this trouble. I'm feeling a little under the weather. The children wouldn't hear of my going along."

The cab was making a U; he signaled wildly. "Wait! . . . Mrs. Holcomb, I've been meaning to talk to you about that old car. I got my license now. I washed it so often it's like I know every inch of it, like it's my car. When you don't need it any more, don't sell it to somebody else first, know what I mean?"

"Oh dear, Myron. You'll have to discuss that with the children."

"Say, are there any trains that go to that place?"

"My God, I don't know if there are any trains going anywhere!" She gave him the name of the town, though, and of the cemetery. ("But how on earth would you find it?")

He nodded his head up and down. "I'll get there."

"Myron," she called—he was already down the steps. "Let me give you the cab fare at least!" Too far away.

"See you next Saturday, to put in those air-conditioners. Fix the lawn," he shouted out the window. "We got to get the place looking nice again."

* * * * *

Leaving the town where the daughters had grown up, passing the railroad station—"Oh, we're going to the station, to meet our relation," they used to sing on their way with their mother to pick him up at the five-fifty-seven—they drove north on the Thruway toward a town where he'd never taken them, only read about, the amateur genealogist, boning up on ancestry at nights, tracing old footsteps from England to New England to Iowa. Completing the final leg of a complicated do-it-your-self project, thanks to the Southern New England Telephone Company, the Hartford Historical Society, the Bank of Connecticut, which was the trustee of the Historical Society, and Miss Joan Addams, the unknown, distant relation who apparently ran the bank.

(Footprints on a beach farther up the coast, ancestors sloshing away from a secondhand passenger ship toward the New World, poison ivy, Indians, and the freedom to be Puritans. Walking on, too—up and down the coast, and then inland, good citizens, settling in towns always just a little away from the major cities. Near Boston, outside Hartford, the other side of Chicago. Fought on the winning side in all the right wars. Never voted for a Democrat, or owned, as far as their descendants knew, a slave or a fortune.)

* * * * *

The local train to Rye left at eleven-five. Myron was on it.

* * * * *

The black hat bobbed up and down on the packages in the back seat of the car as they crested on the Thruway the little industrial cities, outskirting Stamford, Bridgeport, New Haven, views of the Sound, through silver-sided leaves, shiny and turgid from all the rain. Myron, too, saw the Sound and the leaves, through the grimy windows on the eleven-forty-eight express out of Rye.

* * * * *

Pink and white laurel and a summery town. Just as they entered it, the sky cleared completely (to the relief of a hundred brides and their mamas that June wedding day).

* * * * *

Myron tried to grab a hot dog at the New Haven station, but the twelve-forty local left New Haven before he could find a stand.

* * * * *

They ate with good appetites at a yellow-brick inn that looked like a railway station. They had made good time. Then they drove a little east; the road broadened and they saw fully where they were: the Connecticut Valley, tobacco country. Half a mile out of town they saw the spire of the Congregational church. The cemetery, neatly fenced, lay pleasant as a park beside the road. They parked beside the car of their friends.

Far inside, they saw their friends, the other mourners, moving about the land of the dead like tourists or explorers. The smell of new-cut grass, the whir of a power mower; the only other living occupant a grounds keeper in another part of the cemetery keeping up the grounds.

Some pink-and-white wildflowers survived near the entrance, where the newer tombstones were, polished and modern, but not less than five years old. The daughter with the hat put it on as they walked; the other looked through the camera lens, checking the red needle for light: more than enough. The headstones went on like whitecaps on a green sea. Mona Sanders spotted them and waved from way off, life a drowner.

Here and there tall monuments, carved with an angel or a cross or palms and wings, rose above the other stones like buoys. Except for the willows that grew here and there for shade, they were the only tall things in the cemetery. Today they cast no shadows. She adjusted the light meter accordingly.

They converged near the east edge of the cemetery, under the obelisk, highest and oldest of all, conspicuous as a nose and covered with names on four sides, like a list. Stan and Mona both wore dark raincoats, and Mona boots and a pillbox hat with a white feather. "I thought sure the ground would be soaked," she explained in a whisper. "But they didn't get the storm up here."

"What a marvelous old place." They were all whispering.

* * * * *

They walked around the obelisk, reading the names. It stood in the center of a large plot and was surrounded by low tombstones with people's first names, like footnotes to the common markers, in scribed with the full names and dates of everyone below. And, of course, of the mutual Ancestor. The plot was a slightly elevated platform and enclosed by a croquet-wicket iron fence.

Two o'clock. The strains of a motel wedding in the distance. (The train from New Haven slowed down to avoid hitting a child.) Stan looked at his watch and the priest strolled out from around the side of the white church, carrying a purple length of satin over one arm, a silver sprinkler the size of a fountain pen, and a book. He introduced himself. "Father Duffy." They looked at each other expectantly for a moment. "Where is he to go?" one of the daughters asked.

He scrutinized the plot, finally pointing to a faded green mat the same color as the grass in one corner, and lifted it. The men went back to the cars to fetch the envelope, the cardboard box, and the flowers. Underneath the mat, a hole like a square of black paper tacked onto a green rug. A pygmy mine, a black body, which absorbs all radiation and reflects none, a camera, a furnace.

* * * * *

All the green of the cemetery moved with the wind: willow leaves, grass cuttings blown over uncut grass. The tubby priest in his black cassock almost apologetically explained it would be his first interment in a Protestant cemetery. "Not that I'm not ecumenical, mind you." Eye-level with the women, he tilted his head back as one accustomed to addressing taller people; he had a faint white cruciform scar above one eyebrow and perspired slightly. She took a picture of the priest and the others standing at the hole. She turned and photographed the whole cemetery, and the men coming toward them.

"Well, now," said the priest more cheerfully, cuing them. The younger man handed over the cardboard box and the senior daughter took it, warm from sunning in the back seat, removed the silver can and handed the wrappings to someone. Both daughters stepped over the curb separating plot from outside grass; the daughter's husband hesitated, followed, holding the red cross of sweetheart roses and baby's breath. The other couple remained beyond, like witnesses. Unrehearsed, they knelt. Four hands began to lower the canister gently into the hole, but it was too deep, more than an arm's length deep. The can dropped beyond the reach of their hands and fell askew and one of them reached, groped blindly, inefficaciously, to adjust it. They stood, their coatsleeves striped with red earth, and were stung by black-and-tan mosquitoes that instantly came out of the shrubbery to assail the mourners, priest, witnesses.

With his silver pencil the priest sprinkled holy water in the hole and began to read, quickly, about our Brother (but never said his name) who was dead but not forever; Our Father and Jesus his Son who died so that our Brother might live, so his sins could be forgiven. And *Our Father, Hail Mary, May perpetual light shine upon him.* Then he turned and sprinkled the cemetery (as if to Catholicize it) and begged for repose for the souls of all who were buried there, Our Father, Hail Mary. He hurried through a litany, pausing for them to fill in the responses, tardily and faintly. Hear us, O Lord. It was over. There wasn't any dirt to drop into the hole. It was customary, explained the priest, for the grounds keeper to fill in the grave after the family of the departed had left. He'd do it when he finished mowing. They pulled the rug back over the hole, stood at ease, lit cigarettes, smiled.

"It was, well, moving and right, Father," said the daughter with the smear on her right sleeve, after a while. "None of us really are believers. But I think we believed some of what you just said: that he lives because we remember him and the memory is part of us. And he's forgiven, I suppose (forgiveness is harder). You feel guilty about blaming the dead, but you do, and your ceremony makes you realize how human that is. It's up to us to forgive him and grant him the only living he can have now."

The priest batted away at a mosquito as if it were a heresy, and squinted at them, confused by the thought. (This daughter did not have a reputation in her family for tact.) "But your mother said you were Catholics, that you wanted a traditional Catholic ceremony." Then he got it. "You're from New York!" He addressed himself to the group: "You've got pretty big parishes in New York. You lose the personal element. People fall away. Now, here in the country we know everybody in the parish. I might not go so far as to say Mass in this church"—waving toward the white Congregational church—"I'm not *that* ecumenical. But I don't mind reading their social notes. When our flagpole got bent in the storm, the Methodist minister got two of his lads to straighten it out; after all, we can't not have a flag for the Fourth of July." Becoming enthusiastic: "I don't believe in mass Baptism six or eight at a turn. I like to think I know the families; I married the boy and girl. It helps when somebody dies to know the situation. A fine young mother ups and goes suddenly, and her husband, non-Catholic, a skeptic like you, sitting in the hospital bewildered and shocked. The doctors want to do an autopsy. 'What is the Church thinking on that?' he asks me. (I'm doing my rounds there.) I talk to those doctors. Remember, you're dealing with a person. He's not thinking how can I advance the cause of medicine. The man's wife just died, he's got little children, go easy on him. That's how I see myself helping with the human side. That's ecumenicism."

Oh, he had plenty of stories he could tell them about the human side, long practiced in the ceremonies that mark birth, mating, death—anecdotes sad and funny. He remembered one about the double wedding of twins he'd known practically from conception, began to tell it, when the church-lower clock struck.

"Thank you, Father. Thank you so much," they said. He pocketed their offering without looking at it, remarked that he hoped the widow felt easier soon, and ambled away toward the road in his cassock.

"What a fine, simple ceremony," said the mourners.

"Weren't we lucky that it cleared up."

"It was just what he would have wanted. So simple and old and charming."

"Even your mother would have liked it. What a pity."

"Yes. Myron, too. He wanted so much to come."

"Myron? Stan, didn't you tell Myron he could get a ride with us today?"

"No, dear, I'm sure he said he was coming up with them."

Going to meet Daddy on the choo-choo train.

Myron heard the church clock striking as he stepped onto the country platform in his city clothes. Too late now to try and walk, he'd worry about cash to get home later. He asked a cabdriver to take him to the Catholic cemetery.

* * * * *

They posed for a picture under the obelisk, where his name would be inscribed with his ancestors (only the stone turned out to be too soft;

it would be like writing in sand, said the monument-maker, who sold their mother a large footstone instead), and went back, noticing and photographing the graves. Nathaniels and Levis and Suzannas dead for a century or more quietly marking their periods, very old mostly, or very young. Here lay cousin Gaylord six times removed. Great-great-great-great-great-grandfather Deacon Ezekiel, who practiced his deaconry in the Congregational church till he was ninety-seven years old. Naomi and Ruth *aetat* 2 days each, and their mother, Sarah. Worn-out, beloved wives, Revolutionary and Civil warriors, distant relatives, friends and strangers, a whole family wiped out by diphtheria, graves designated with little Historical Society metal crosses, modern townsfolk with perpetual plastic bouquets.

* * * * *

Myron's cabdriver asked directions of a cop, who guided them by mistake to the Catholic rectory. The priest, returning from marrying off a couple of parishioners, found him ringing the bell and stood with him by the Gothic door as he inquired about Mr. Holcomb. "Yes, yes," said the priest, hot in his cassock. "The name does ring a bell."

"People in a big green car? I was going to ride back with them. I've got to talk to them about buying it. Mr. Holcomb said it was like my car. You know the people I mean?"

The little priest scratched at a mosquito bite on his right temple. Holcomb . . . Holcomb . . . He's on the—um, left as you go in, I think, halfway back there, behind the church. I can't point out the spot because it's almost time for Benediction. Come join us when you've finished, if you'd like. Yes, we buried him last week."

"Mr. Holcomb would have liked for me to have that car."

"The family will be touched, son."

Myron satisfied himself with a long survey of the cemetery from the outside—the squat granite monuments; in there somewhere, the old man. The place could have used a good mowing. He began to walk toward where he could hitch a ride, make a phone call, get a beer.

He was, therefore, the only interested party to miss hearing the crack like a pistol shot. Nearing the cemetery entrance, the other mourners looked up, over to where their cars were parked. Slowly, cleanly, an oak branch as big itself as a tree was separating itself from the oak, and dropped like a feather through a windless sky toward the green Oldsmobile.

Their mouths fell open. The car horn let loose a piercing, drawn-out wail. Splinters and pebbles and shards of shatterproof glass rose like drops from a rain puddle. A lengthy tearing and rending of wood, twigs, bark, metal, leaves, while the branch heaved turbulently, until gradually the leaves and twigs arranged themselves around the car, like camouflage. One branch had gone through the left-hand side window; the others, miraculously, were intact. The roof was trepanned.

Behind them, the son of the grounds keeper continued to play war among the graves, the noise of the falling branch drowning out his quiet *pkow*. He lifted a corner of the mat to see what lay under the roses.

* * * * *

Soul wished that Body would erupt, blow the lid, whirl out of the black hole like a tornado of ashes, take shape, take substance, divide into limbs, plant them on the ground, stride away. He hadn't meant the separation to be so complete, not so final.

What if they came up the long driveway under the pines, and he heard them in his upstairs bedroom and were there, back from that place, sick but undead, pale and alive? Or if he greeted them in his garden, working among the roses—"Guess how much rain we had!" And they'd have to go through it all over again. After the effort, the work that goes into burying a dead man. Could they endure having him back again, after that?

Julie Hayden was born in New York City in 1939, the daughter of the Pulitzer-prize-winning poet Phyllis McGinley and Bill Hayden, a public relations analyst at Bell Telephone. She served on the editorial staff of *The New Yorker* from 1965 until her death at age 42 and all but two of the stories in this collection first appeared in that publication. She was at work on a novel at the time of her death but *The Lists of the Past* remains her only published work.

Cheryl Strayed is the author of the #1 *New York Times* bestseller *Wild: From Lost to Found on the Pacific Crest Trail*, *The New York Times* bestseller *Tiny Beautiful Things*, and the novel *Torch*. *Wild* was chosen by Oprah Winfrey as her first selection for Oprah's Book Club 2.0 and optioned for film by Reese Witherspoon's production company, Pacific Standard. *Wild* was selected as the winner of the Barnes & Noble Discover Award, the Indie Choice Award, an Oregon Book Award, a Pacific Northwest Booksellers Award, and a Midwest Booksellers Choice Award. Her books have been translated into twenty-eight languages around the world. She lives in Portland, Oregon with her husband and their two children. More at www.cherylstrayed.com.

More Titles From Pharos Editions

The Lists of the Past by Julie Hayden
SELECTED AND INTRODUCED BY CHERYL STRAYED

The Tattooed Heart & *My Name Is Rose* by Theodora Keogh
SELECTED AND INTRODUCED BY LIDIA YUKNAVITCH

Total Loss Farm: A Year in the Life by Raymond Mungo
SELECTED AND INTRODUCED BY DANA SPIOTTA

Crazy Weather by Charles L McNichols
SELECTED AND INTRODUCED BY URSULA K LE GUIN

Inside Moves by Todd Walton
SELECTED AND INTRODUCED BY SHERMAN ALEXIE

McTeague: A Story of San Francisco by Frank Norris
SELECTED AND INTRODUCED BY JONATHAN EVISON

You Play the Black and the Red Comes Up by Richard Hallas
SELECTED AND INTRODUCED BY MATT GROENING

The Land of Plenty by Robert Cantwell
SELECTED AND INTRODUCED BY JESS WALTER